Introduction

They say monsters come at night.
But no one ever warned me how beau

I stepped into the dark to destroy the beasts who ruined my life—
and instead found a throne of shadows,
a hunger I didn't expect,
and three vampire lords who see me not as prey... but as the prize.

Their world is carved from silk and steel.
A place where power tastes like blood on the tongue,
where desire bites deeper than any fang,
and where the most dangerous thing I could lose... is myself.

I came with a blade and a vendetta.
But what happens when your body betrays your vengeance?
When the monster you hate is the only one who sees you?

This is not a fairytale.
There are no heroes here.
Only games.
Only ruin.
Only the girl who dared to walk into hell—and smiled when it bit back.

Welcome to the choosing.
Make sure you survive long enough to regret it.

for breakfast.
But life has other plans.

And honestly?
I think I'm about to break every single one of them.

Table of contents:

Chapter 1: The Price of Blood 5
Chapter 2: Marked for Selection 12
Chapter 3: His Rules, My Game 19
Chapter 4: The Chamber of Lies 26
Chapter 5: Silk and Steel 33
Chapter 6: The Dance Begins 38
Chapter 7: Blood and Banter 44
Chapter 8: Test of Pain, Taste of Power 49
Chapter 9: The Monster Beneath the Mask 57
Chapter 10: Secrets Written in Bone 62
Chapter 11: A Bed Made of Chains 69
Chapter 12: Feeding the Flame 75
Chapter 13: The Price of Defiance 83
Chapter 14: When Silence Screams 90
Chapter 15: Beneath His Thirst 97
Chapter 16: My Name on His Tongue 102
Chapter 17: The Bite I Didn't Hate 107
Chapter 18: What the Mirror Reveals 112
Chapter 19: A Dress to Kill In 119
Chapter 20: Before the Blade Strikes 124
Chapter 21: The Truth Buried in Blood 129
Chapter 22: A Thirst Older Than Vengeance 133
Chapter 23: Kiss Before Betrayal 139
Chapter 24: Marked by Fire, Not Fangs 143

Chapter 25: The Undoing Begins 149
Chapter 26: The Throne Isn't Empty 154
Chapter 27: His Bite, My Undoing 160
Chapter 28: The Girl Who Walked Into Hell 165
Chapter 29: Ashes of What I Was 169
Chapter 30: The Queen of the Unbroken 174

His Bite, My Undoing

Author: Lilith Ravelle

Copyright © 2025 by : Lilith Ravelle
All rights reserved.
No part of this publication may be reproduced, distributed, or transmitted in any form or by any means—electronic, mechanical, photocopying, recording, or otherwise—without the prior written permission of the publisher, except in the case of brief quotations used in reviews, articles, or scholarly work.

This is a work of fiction. Names, characters, places, and incidents are either products of the author's imagination or used fictitiously. Any resemblance to actual events, locales, or persons—living or dead—is entirely coincidental.
First Edition

Chapter 1: The Price of Blood

The scent of despair was a sickly-sweet perfume in the air, clinging to the silk drapes and the polished marble. It was a familiar aroma, one Lyra Virellan had worn for years, like a second skin. Tonight, however, it mingled with something else – the cloying metallic tang of fear and something far more primal. Blood.

Twelve of us, they called us. Twelve offerings. Twelve lambs to the slaughter. We stood in a cavernous chamber, bathed in the anemic glow of ancient, enchanted crystals embedded in the vaulted ceiling. Their light, a pale, ethereal blue, made everyone look like ghosts, save for the vibrant splash of crimson Lyra had foolishly, or perhaps defiantly, chosen for her lips.

A ripple went through the line of girls beside her – a soft gasp, a tremor of a hand, a barely suppressed sob. Lyra remained as still as the ancient statues guarding the entrance, her spine a rod of iron. She focused on the intricate patterns of the mosaic floor, a dizzying spiral of gold and black that seemed to draw you down into its depths. *Don't show weakness,* a voice, her mother's voice, whispered in her mind. *They feed on it.*

And feed they would. This wasn't a choice; it was a debt. A blood debt, paid in flesh. Her family's blood, shed by them, demanded this payment. Her presence here was not surrender, but infiltration. A calculated sacrifice, the first step in a long, deadly game.

A low, guttural murmur echoed from the far end of the chamber, cutting through the heavy silence. The vampires. They had arrived.

Lyra risked a glance. They emerged from shadows that seemed to coil and writhe around them, each a living sculpture of dangerous grace. Their movements were fluid, predatory, like sharks gliding through deep water. Cloaks of darkest velvet billowed, revealing glimpses of tailored suits beneath, stark against skin that seemed impossibly pale. Their eyes, even from this distance, gleamed with an unsettling intensity, ranging from the predatory crimson of fresh kill to the ancient, bottomless depths of obsidian.

Her gaze snagged on one figure, taller than the rest, who moved with an almost insolent ease. He didn't just walk; he commanded the air around him. His hair, dark as a raven's wing, framed a face carved from stone – sharp cheekbones, a strong jaw, and lips that were a cruel, perfect curve. But it was his eyes that held her, even across the vast distance of the hall. They were the color of molten gold, burning with an internal fire that promised both destruction and a terrifying kind of allure. Cassian. The name, whispered in the hushed, fearful tales of mortals, tasted like ash on her tongue. The monster she had come to kill.

A nervous fidget from the girl to Lyra's left broke her trance. The girl, no older than Lyra herself, with wide, frightened eyes the color of a summer sky, looked about to faint. Lyra felt a flicker of pity, quickly extinguished. Pity was a luxury she couldn't afford. It blurred the lines, softened the resolve. And tonight, her resolve had to be sharper than any blade.

The High Priestess, a gaunt, ancient vampire woman whose voice crackled like dry leaves, began the ritual. Her words were ancient, forgotten incantations, weaving a tapestry of subservience and sacrifice. Lyra listened, every sense alert, cataloging the nuances of the ritual, searching for a weakness, an opening.

"You have been chosen," the Priestess intoned, her voice echoing in the vast space. "Chosen to serve. Chosen to give. Chosen to… pleasure." A collective shiver ran through the line of offerings. "Your purpose is simple: to sate the Thirst. To ease the ancient hunger of our Lords. To be… consumed."

Lyra's lip twitched. *Consumed, huh? Not if I consume you first.*

Her gaze drifted back to Cassian. He wasn't looking at the Priestess, or at the other Lords. His golden eyes were fixed on the line of girls, sweeping slowly, deliberately, over each one. When his gaze landed on Lyra, a spark ignited. It wasn't just interest; it was recognition, or perhaps, a challenge. He paused, his head tilting ever so slightly, as if he could smell the defiance simmering beneath her carefully constructed calm.

A wave of heat washed over Lyra, not from fear, but from a strange, unsettling awareness. It was as if his gaze was a physical touch, tracing the line of her throat, the curve of her collarbone. She held his stare, refusing to look away, a silent dare. Let him see. Let him know she wasn't just another cowering lamb.

The Priestess continued her droning incantation, now addressing the vampire Lords directly. "My Lords, choose your first taste. Let the blood sing its song of surrender."

A few of the other Lords, less patient or perhaps more direct, stepped forward, their eyes settling on the girls who appeared most fragile, most afraid. Lyra watched as a pale, willowy girl was gently, yet firmly, guided away by a vampire with eyes like chipped ice. The girl's silent tears were the only protest.

Then, Cassian moved. He didn't stride; he flowed, like mercury, directly towards the line. Every other girl stiffened, their fear a palpable wave. Lyra's heart beat a steady rhythm, refusing to accelerate. She maintained eye contact as he approached, his golden eyes blazing, a predatory smirk playing on his lips.

He stopped directly in front of her. His height was imposing, casting a long shadow that enveloped her. She had to tilt her head back to meet his gaze, and even then, she felt dwarfed by his sheer presence. He smelled of old leather, something metallic, and an undertone of primal danger that was both terrifying and, to her surprise, oddly captivating.

He didn't touch her. Not yet. But his hand, strong and elegant, hovered inches from her cheek, his long fingers flexing slightly. His eyes, now closer, were even more intense, searching, dissecting. He wasn't just looking at her; he was looking *into* her, peeling back the layers.

"Interesting," he murmured, his voice a low, resonant growl that vibrated through the very floor. It was a voice that could coax secrets from stone and send shivers down the spine. "No fear."

Lyra held his gaze. "Fear is a waste of time," she replied, her voice steady, even. A subtle challenge in her tone.

His lips curved into a wider, more dangerous smile, revealing just a hint of pearly white fangs. "Oh, I assure you, little mortal, fear has its uses. It sharpens the senses. It sweetens the blood." His eyes dropped to her lips, the defiant crimson she had chosen. "Red. A bold choice."

A thought flashed through Lyra's mind, unbidden and slightly absurd: *I really shouldn't have worn red lipstick when I was about to be picked for dinner.* The absurdity of it made a tiny, almost imperceptible twitch at the corner of her own lips.

Cassian caught it. His golden eyes narrowed, a flicker of surprise mixed with something else – amusement? He leaned in closer, his breath, cool and faintly minty, ghosting across her face. "Amusement, little mortal? When faced with your fate?"

"It seemed appropriate," Lyra said, her voice a shade softer, playing the game. "Better to face it with a smile than with tears."

He let out a low chuckle, a sound that was surprisingly rich and genuinely amused. It sent a strange tremor through Lyra, not of fear, but of… something akin to an electric current. This was not the mindless beast she had imagined. This was a calculating, intelligent predator. And he was enjoying this.

"You intrigue me," he finally said, his voice dropping to an intimate whisper. "Which is precisely why… you will be mine first."

He reached out, his long fingers brushing against the pulse point on her neck. It was a light touch, almost tender, yet it was filled with an implicit promise of possession. Lyra felt a jolt, a strange mix of dread and a frisson of something she couldn't quite name. His touch was cold, yet it sparked a peculiar heat beneath her skin. This was it. The first contact. The marking. Not yet the bite, but the claim.

He held her gaze, his golden eyes burning into hers, asserting his dominance. "You will be brought to me," he commanded, his voice returning to its resonant tone, a public declaration. "Tonight."

He then straightened, turning his back on her, his powerful frame radiating an aura of absolute authority. The other Lords glanced at him, a mixture of respect and perhaps a hint of envy in their expressions. Cassian had made his choice, and it was clear he tolerated no arguments.

As he walked away, a low, collective sigh went through the remaining girls – a mix of relief and renewed terror. Lyra, however, felt only a surge of grim satisfaction. It had worked. She was in. She was marked. The game had truly begun.

A silent, cloaked vampire, one of the castle's guards, stepped forward and gestured for Lyra to follow. She cast one last glance at the mosaic floor, at the dizzying spiral. *Into the labyrinth,* she thought, a cold resolve settling deep in her bones. *Let's see who gets lost first.*

She walked out of the chamber, her head held high, leaving behind the fear and the faint scent of despair, and carrying with her the burning determination of vengeance. She was Lyra Virellan, and she had just walked into hell, not as a victim, but as a weapon.

Chapter 2: Marked for Selection

The guard, a hulking figure with eyes like chips of flint, led Lyra through a labyrinth of dimly lit corridors. The air grew colder with every turn, carrying the faint, earthy scent of ancient stone and something else – something almost sweet, yet chillingly antiseptic. This castle wasn't just old; it felt alive, breathing with a dark, slumbering power. Lyra's senses, heightened by adrenaline and years of honed survival instincts, absorbed every detail: the subtle shift in the air currents, the way the shadows danced in the flickering torchlight, the unnerving silence broken only by the soft pad of their footsteps.

They passed grand arches and heavy, studded oak doors, each one hinting at forgotten secrets within. Lyra knew from her research that Sinful Castle, as it was chillingly named, was an architectural monstrosity built over centuries by a succession of vampire lords, each adding their own layer of twisted grandeur. It was a fortress, a prison, and a mausoleum, all rolled into one. And tonight, it was her temporary home.

Her mind raced, cataloging, planning. The objective was simple: survive, gather information, and find a way to strike. Cassian had chosen her first. That was both a blessing and a curse. A blessing because it gave her direct access to the most powerful vampire in the castle, potentially the one responsible for her family's demise. A curse because it put her directly in the line of fire, under the microscopic scrutiny of a predator far more cunning than she'd anticipated. His amusement back in the chamber had rattled her, just a little. He saw something in her, something beyond the fear. And that made him dangerous.

They finally stopped before a towering door of dark, polished wood, ornate carvings swirling across its surface like frozen vines. The guard pushed it open, revealing a chamber that was both opulent and stark. It wasn't a bedchamber in the traditional sense, more like a waiting room for... what?

The room was vast, dominated by a large, circular stone plinth in the center, encircled by several heavy, iron-wrought chairs. Tapestries depicting hunting scenes – of men, not deer – adorned the walls, their faded colors adding to the somber atmosphere. A single, flickering candelabrum on a small table provided the only light, casting long, dancing shadows. There was no bed, no comforts. Just the plinth and the chairs.

"Wait here," the guard rumbled, his voice devoid of emotion. He gestured towards one of the chairs. "The Lord will be with you shortly."

He left, the heavy door thudding shut behind him, plunging the room into an oppressive silence. Lyra walked to the plinth, running her fingers over its smooth, cold surface. It felt like an altar. She chose one of the chairs, positioning herself so she could see the door and the entire room. She sat, not slumping, but poised, ready. Her hand instinctively went to the small, concealed blade she wore strapped to her inner thigh, hidden beneath the flowing fabric of the simple dress she'd been given upon arrival – a plain, dark gray shift that offered no advantages. She hadn't been frisked. An oversight, or a deliberate choice? She decided to assume the latter. They were arrogant. Good. Arrogance bred carelessness.

Minutes stretched into an eternity. Each tick of an invisible clock seemed to amplify the silence, pressing down on her. She forced herself to breathe deeply, evenly, slowing her pulse. She wasn't afraid. Fear would only betray her. Her mind, however, was a whirlwind of calculations. What would Cassian want? Blood, yes. But something else, too. His eyes had betrayed an interest that went beyond simple hunger.

A soft click of the door. Lyra's senses snapped to full alert. Cassian entered, not with the dramatic flair he displayed in the main hall, but with a quiet, almost domestic casualness that was somehow even more unsettling. He wore a loose-fitting black silk shirt, open at the collar, revealing the strong column of his throat and a hint of corded muscle. His dark trousers were tailored to perfection. He looked less like a monstrous overlord and more like a dangerous man returning to his private domain. Which, Lyra supposed, was exactly what he was.

His golden eyes, now no longer blazing with public display, held a calculating glint as they swept over her, taking in her posture, her stillness. He didn't smile this time. Just watched.

He didn't speak. Instead, he walked towards a small, ornate cabinet in the corner of the room. He poured himself a clear liquid from a decanter into a crystal goblet. It wasn't blood;

it was too pale. Some kind of fine liquor, Lyra surmised. He took a slow sip, his gaze never leaving her.

The silence lengthened, stretching tautly between them, vibrating with unspoken tension. Lyra refused to break it. She would not be the first to speak. She would not give him the satisfaction of seeing her unnerved.

Finally, he set the goblet down, the faint clink echoing loudly in the stillness. He began to circle her, his movements slow, deliberate, like a predator stalking its prey. He passed behind her, and Lyra felt the subtle shift in the air, the faint scent of him growing stronger. She resisted the urge to turn her head, keeping her gaze fixed straight ahead.

"Still no fear?" he purred, his voice a low rumble from behind her, inches from her ear. The hairs on her arms prickled. "Or are you simply very good at hiding it?"

Lyra remained silent.

He chuckled, a soft, dry sound. "A defiant one. I like that." He moved back into her line of sight, stopping directly in front of her. His eyes were no longer molten gold, but a rich amber, deep and reflective. "Most of them scream. Or cry. Or plead." He leaned down, his face mere inches from hers. "You, little mortal, simply wait."

"Waiting is a strategy," Lyra replied, her voice cool and level.

His eyebrows, dark and perfectly sculpted, rose slightly. "Indeed. And what strategy might that be?"

"To observe," she said, meeting his gaze without flinching. "To understand. To learn the rules of the game."

A slow, predatory smile spread across his face, revealing the tips of his fangs, sharper and more pronounced now. "Ah. So you think this is a game." He straightened up, walked to the plinth, and placed his palms flat on its surface. "Tell me, little mortal, what do you think the rules are?"

"Your rules," Lyra stated simply. "But I intend to make them my game."

He let out a soft, almost soundless laugh. "Bold. Reckless. And perhaps… foolish." He pushed off the plinth, resuming his slow pacing. "You know why you are here, Lyra Virellan."

The use of her full name, spoken in his rich, deep voice, was a jolt. He knew her. Of course, he would. They always did their research. But hearing it from *him* felt different, like a possessive mark.

"I am here to pay a debt," she said, her voice betraying nothing.

"A blood debt," he corrected, his voice hardening. "Your family's debt." His gaze turned sharp, piercing. "Do you remember how your father screamed?"

The question was a calculated blow, aimed directly at her most vulnerable point. Lyra felt a cold wave wash over her, a familiar phantom ache in her chest. She closed her eyes for a fleeting second, just long enough to push the image away, to rebuild the wall around her emotions. When she opened them, her eyes were cold, devoid of the pain she felt within.

"I remember everything," she said, her voice flat.

Cassian watched her, his expression unreadable. He seemed to be searching for something, a crack in her composure. "Good," he murmured. "Memory can be a powerful tool. Or a powerful weapon."

He stopped pacing, standing still a few feet from her. "Tonight, Lyra Virellan, you will be tested. Tested not just for your blood, but for your… spirit." He walked towards the plinth again, standing beside it, his gaze fixed on her. "Come here."

Lyra hesitated for a fraction of a second. She didn't like being commanded, but defiance now would gain her nothing. She rose gracefully from the chair and walked towards the plinth, stopping opposite him. The cold stone felt like an invitation to sacrifice.

"Place your hands on the plinth," he instructed, his voice soft but firm.

Lyra placed her hands flat on the cold stone, mirroring his posture. His golden eyes tracked her every movement.

"Feel it?" he asked, his voice low. "The history. The power. The countless lives that have… ended here." His words were a subtle threat, a reminder of her precarious position.

Lyra looked at him, her gaze unwavering. "I feel cold stone," she retorted, a hint of dry sarcasm in her voice.

A genuine smirk, full of wicked amusement, touched his lips again. "You are truly unlike any other, Lyra Virellan. Most would be trembling." He leaned in, his voice dropping to a near whisper. "Tell me, little mortal, what frightens you most?"

Lyra paused, considering. She couldn't tell him the truth – that the thought of failing, of her family's sacrifice being in vain, was her greatest fear. She needed to give him an answer that would disarm him, or at least amuse him further.

A mischievous glint entered her eyes. "Actually," she said, her voice light, "my greatest fear is a dinner party without proper cutlery. Imagine having to eat steak with your bare hands. Barbaric."

Cassian stared at her for a long moment, his golden eyes widening almost imperceptibly. Then, a low chuckle escaped him, building into a full, throaty laugh that filled the silent chamber. It was a surprising sound, deep and resonant, not the sinister cackle she might have expected from a creature of the night. It was the sound of genuine, unbridled amusement.

"A dinner party," he repeated, still chuckling, shaking his head slightly. "You are truly... unique." He took a step closer, his hand reaching out, not to her throat, but to her chin. His touch was cold, yet electric, tipping her face up so her gaze was locked with his.

"Tonight, Lyra Virellan," he said, his voice now serious again, though a hint of the amusement still lingered in his eyes. "You will learn that some meals are meant to be savored, not cut."

His thumb brushed lightly over her lower lip, a subtle, almost possessive gesture. "And I intend to savor every drop."

The air crackled between them, thick with unspoken promise and veiled threat. Lyra felt a peculiar tension, a strange mix of apprehension and a primal, almost forbidden curiosity. This wasn't just about blood. This was about power, control, and a dangerous game of cat and mouse where the lines between hunter and hunted were blurring even before the first bite.

His golden eyes held hers, a silent declaration. **She was marked for selection.** Not just for his hunger, but for something far more complex. And Lyra knew, with a chilling certainty, that her journey into the heart of Sinful Castle had only just begun. The price of blood was not just payment; it was an invitation.

Chapter 3: His Rules, My Game

Lyra was led from the antechamber not to a dungeon, as a part of her had grimly anticipated, but to a lavish suite nestled deep within the castle. It was an odd juxtaposition – the brutal, cold ceremony of selection followed by what appeared to be a gilded cage. But a cage it was, nonetheless.

The rooms were furnished with heavy, antique pieces: a massive four-poster bed draped in dark velvet, a fireplace with a roaring fire that did little to dispel the underlying chill, and a sitting area with plush armchairs. The walls were adorned with intricate tapestries depicting scenes of what Lyra recognized as the ancient Vampire Wars, full of blood and triumph. It was a subtle, constant reminder of who held the power here.

A young, silent vampire servant, with eyes like polished obsidian, waited for her. He gestured towards a wardrobe carved from dark, gleaming wood. Inside hung a selection of dresses, each one more opulent and less practical than the last. They were clearly designed not for comfort or concealment, but for display. For the "offerings."

"His Lordship requests you prepare for the evening's gathering," the servant's voice was a low murmur, barely audible. He placed a small, silver tray on a nearby table, laden with perfumes, lotions, and a selection of delicate jewelry.

Lyra suppressed a sigh. *I came here to kill people. Not to do a bloody fashion lookbook.* The thought, so absurd in the grim circumstances, almost made her crack a smile. But she kept her face carefully blank. Every interaction was a test, every expression a potential tell.

"Very well," she said, her voice even. "Is there anything else?"

The servant inclined his head slightly. "Lord Cassian will send for you when he is ready." With that, he vanished as silently as he had appeared, leaving Lyra alone in the opulent prison.

She walked to the large window. It was barred, of course, with intricate wrought iron work that looked more decorative than restrictive, but it was sturdy nonetheless. Below, the castle grounds stretched out, a manicured but foreboding landscape. Distant lights twinkled in what must be other parts of the sprawling fortress, and beyond that, nothing but the endless, dark forest. Escape, she knew, would be no simple feat.

Lyra methodically inspected the room. She checked beneath the bed, behind the tapestries, and inside the wardrobe. No hidden passages, no obvious weaknesses. The fireplace flue was too narrow. She even ran her hand over the stone walls, searching for loose bricks, but found nothing. The castle was built to hold, not to release.

Her gaze fell on the dresses. She sighed. This was part of the game, a ritual of subservience. They wanted her to look like a docile offering. Fine. She would play along. For now. She chose a dark emerald green gown, its fabric a rich, heavy silk that shimmered with every movement. It had a high neckline but was cut to flatter her figure, hinting at curves without being overtly revealing. It felt like armor, a subtle defiance in its elegance. It was also long enough to conceal the small blade still strapped to her thigh. An important detail.

As she dressed, her mind worked furiously. Cassian had called this a "game." That meant rules, objectives, and potentially, winning conditions. She needed to understand his motivation beyond simple hunger. His amusement, his challenge, suggested something deeper. Was this a test of spirit, as he'd said? A way to find a partner, or merely a more interesting plaything?

She carefully applied a minimal amount of the scented lotion and perfume. She didn't want to mask her natural scent, the scent that had drawn Cassian, but she also didn't want to appear unkempt. The scent of fear was powerful, but so was the scent of a woman who carried herself with quiet confidence. She reapplied her crimson lipstick, a small act of rebellion. Let him remember the "bold choice."

Time stretched on, marked only by the shifting shadows in the room. Lyra used the time to meditate, to center herself, to review her knowledge of vampire lore and the few scraps of information she had about the ruling House of Sinful. They were ancient, powerful, and notoriously cruel. Arkyn, the patriarch, was rarely seen, a shadow pulling strings from the deepest recesses of the castle. Lorcan, the quiet observer, was known for his intellect and his chillingly calm demeanor. And then there was Cassian, the dominant, the brutal, the one who had marked her.

A soft knock interrupted her thoughts. The same silent servant entered. "His Lordship is ready."

Lyra took a deep breath, her hands briefly clenching into fists at her sides, then relaxing. This was it. The next phase.

She followed the servant through a different set of corridors, even grander than the last. These were lit by sconces holding hundreds of flickering candles, casting a warm, deceptive glow on walls covered in priceless tapestries and paintings of ancestral vampire lords, their eyes seeming to follow her. The air grew warmer, infused with the scent of roasted meats, fine wines, and, subtly, blood. This was where the "gathering" would take place.

They stopped before an immense, double-door of black iron, etched with an intricate, terrifying crest of a bat with outstretched wings, its fangs dripping. The servant pushed the doors open, revealing a dazzling spectacle.

The room was a ballroom, but unlike any Lyra had ever seen. The ceiling soared, painted with constellations that seemed to shift and twinkle. Crystal chandeliers hung like frozen waterfalls, refracting light into a million shimmering facets. Tables laden with exotic foods and goblets brimming with dark red liquid – blood, no doubt – lined the perimeter. A live orchestra played a haunting, classical piece that filled the space.

And the people. Dozens of vampires, all dressed in opulent finery, mingled and conversed, their voices a low hum. They were beautiful, dangerously so, with an aura of ancient power that made the air thrum. Lyra saw other "offerings" among them, girls in equally elaborate gowns, some looking terrified, others attempting to blend in, to appear composed. Their eyes, however, all held the same vulnerability.

Then she saw him. Cassian. He stood near a raised dais at the far end of the room, flanked by two other male vampires. One was Lorcan, immediately recognizable by his quiet stillness, his dark, watchful eyes. He seemed almost a part of the shadows, observing everything. The other was an older, more imposing figure, though Lyra couldn't immediately place him. His presence exuded an ancient, almost suffocating authority. This must be Arkyn. Or perhaps another high-ranking Lord.

Cassian's golden eyes found her instantly as she entered, a spark of recognition flashing in their depths. He didn't smile, but a subtle tightening around his lips indicated his awareness. He had been waiting.

Lyra walked into the room, her spine straight, her chin slightly raised. She ignored the curious glances, the subtle shifts in conversation as she passed. She was here, not as a guest, but as an unwilling participant, and she carried herself with the cold dignity of one who had nothing left to lose.

As she made her way through the periphery of the crowd, Lyra took mental notes. This was not just a social gathering; it was a display of power, a vetting process. The other girls, their fear radiating like heat, were already being assessed by the vampires.

A vampire, sleek and elegant, with eyes the color of emeralds, approached one of the other offerings, a trembling blonde girl. He spoke to her in a low, coaxing tone, then gently, possessively, took her arm and led her away towards a more secluded alcove. The girl's eyes were wide with terror.

Lyra felt a flicker of grim satisfaction. Let them think she was like the others. Let them underestimate her.

Suddenly, a presence was beside her. Cassian. He had moved with such silent speed that she hadn't even heard him approach.

"Enjoying the festivities, little mortal?" His voice was a low purr, meant only for her ears, yet it carried an undertone of dangerous amusement.

Lyra turned her head slowly, meeting his gaze. He was closer than she'd anticipated, his scent – metallic, musky, utterly vampire – filling her senses. She could feel the subtle warmth radiating from his body, the latent power contained within.

"It's certainly… lively," she replied, keeping her tone neutral.

He chuckled, a soft, dry sound. "Lively indeed. We like to make our guests feel welcome." His golden eyes dropped to her emerald dress, appreciating the fabric, the cut. "A fine choice. It suits you."

"I'm glad you approve," Lyra said, a hint of sarcasm she hoped he wouldn't catch.

He did. His smile widened, a flash of white fangs. "Oh, I do. Very much." He leaned in closer, his voice dropping to a seductive whisper. "Tell me, Lyra. What rules do you believe govern this little gathering?"

Lyra looked around the opulent ballroom, at the beautiful, deadly creatures mingling within. She met his gaze directly. "Survival of the fittest, I suppose," she said, her voice steady. "And the strongest bite wins."

He let out a low, appreciative hum, his eyes gleaming. "An astute observation. But perhaps," he paused, his gaze intensifying, "there are other rules you have yet to discover. Rules that govern… desire. And devotion."

His meaning was clear. This wasn't just about survival. It was about submission. About becoming something more than an offering.

Lyra held his gaze, a small, defiant smile playing on her lips. "Then I suppose I'll just have to break a few to find out."

Cassian laughed again, a genuine, delighted sound that seemed to surprise even some of the nearby vampires. He shook his head, a glimmer of admiration in his golden eyes. "You truly are something, Lyra Virellan. Something… exquisite."

He extended a hand, his touch light as he grazed her bare arm. "Come. The dance begins."

Lyra felt a shiver, not of fear, but of anticipation. She was playing his game, in his castle, by his rules. But she had her own agenda, her own secret weapons. And she intended to use them all. The hunt was on.

Chapter 4: The Chamber of Lies

The ballroom was a whirlwind of dark cloaks and glittering jewels, a deceptive facade of elegance masking the raw hunger beneath. Lyra moved through the crowd with Cassian at her side, his presence a magnetic force that parted the sea of vampires. Their eyes, a kaleidoscope of ancient malice and cold curiosity, followed her every step. Some were clearly envious of Cassian's choice, others merely assessing the new "toy" in the Master's hands.

Cassian led her past tables laden with exotic dishes, past whispers and veiled glances, until they reached a secluded alcove bathed in the glow of a single, intricately carved lamp. Waiting there was Lorcan.

He stood perfectly still, a statue of quiet power. His dark hair fell over a face that was handsome in a more austere, classic way than Cassian's fierce beauty. His eyes, the color of twilight, were deep and knowing, holding a profound sadness that seemed to contradict the ruthless nature of his kind. He wore a simple, dark tunic that emphasized his lean, athletic build. There was an aura of stillness about him, a sense of immense patience that was almost more unnerving than Cassian's overt dominance.

"Brother," Cassian greeted, his voice losing some of its playful edge, becoming sharper, more formal.

Lorcan inclined his head slightly. "Cassian. And your... guest." His gaze settled on Lyra, cool and assessing, lingering for a moment longer than necessary. Unlike Cassian, there was no overt amusement in his eyes, only a quiet, penetrating intensity that felt like a probe.

"Lyra Virellan," Cassian introduced, his hand coming to rest lightly on the small of Lyra's back, a possessive gesture that made her skin tingle with a strange awareness. "She possesses a... refreshing lack of fear."

Lorcan's lips curved into a faint, almost imperceptible smile. "Indeed. A rare trait in our... modern acquisitions." His voice was a low, smooth baritone, calm and measured, like the surface of a deep, still lake.

Lyra met his gaze evenly. She sensed a profound intelligence behind those twilight eyes. He wasn't just observing her; he was analyzing, dissecting.

"Lorcan has a fondness for… puzzles," Cassian said, his voice laced with a hint of warning, or perhaps a challenge. "Especially those with sharp edges."

"And Lyra seems to be an enigma wrapped in defiance," Lorcan countered, his eyes never leaving hers. "A fascinating combination."

"Enough pleasantries," Cassian interjected, a slight edge to his voice. "Lorcan wishes to… converse with you, Lyra. Alone."

Lyra felt a jolt. This was unexpected. A separate interrogation. "Why?" she asked, her voice calm, direct.

Cassian's gaze was sharp. "Because he can. And because… he wishes to." His hand on her back tightened infinitesimally. "Humor him. It would be wise."

He gave her a pointed look, a silent command. Lyra understood. This was another test. A chance to gauge her wit, her composure, her willingness to submit. Or, more accurately, her ability to *appear* to submit.

Cassian stepped back, disappearing into the swirling crowd as silently as he had arrived. Lyra was left alone with Lorcan, in the quiet solitude of the alcove, the festive sounds of the ballroom fading into a distant hum.

Lorcan gestured to a small, ornate chaise lounge positioned against the wall. "Please, have a seat."

Lyra chose a high-backed armchair instead, deliberately positioning herself for a clear view of the entrance and

Lorcan. She didn't want to appear too comfortable, too relaxed. This was still enemy territory.

Lorcan settled onto the chaise, his posture relaxed, yet his eyes remained intensely focused on her. He exuded an unnerving calm, like a coiled viper.

"So," he began, his voice soft. "Cassian finds you... intriguing. That is unusual. He rarely deviates from the predictable."

"And you, Lord Lorcan?" Lyra asked, returning his directness. "Do you find me predictable?"

A faint smile touched his lips again. "Not yet. But the night is young. And most mortals, when faced with true power, reveal their predictable patterns of fear and desire."

"Perhaps I am not most mortals," Lyra countered.

"Indeed." He paused, his gaze sweeping over her, not with Cassian's raw hunger, but with an almost academic curiosity. "Tell me, Lyra Virellan, if you were to define yourself in one word, what would it be?"

Lyra considered. She couldn't say 'vengeful' or 'assassin'. "Resilient," she said simply.

"Resilient," Lorcan echoed, tasting the word. "An admirable quality. But resilience can be broken. Or bent." He leaned forward slightly, his voice dropping to a confidential whisper. "Tell me, Lyra, do you believe in fate?"

The question caught her off guard. It wasn't about power or fear. It was philosophical. "I believe we make our own fate," she replied, her voice firm.

"Ah, the illusion of free will," Lorcan murmured, a hint of melancholy in his tone. "A comforting lie for mortals. But what if your path was set long before you drew your first breath? What if your very presence here was… inevitable?"

Lyra felt a prickle of unease. His words were designed to disarm, to plant seeds of doubt. "I don't believe in inevitability when there's a choice to be made."

"Even if the choice leads you to the same destination?" he challenged softly. "Imagine a maze, Lyra. You choose left, then right, then left again. You believe you are making choices, but all paths ultimately lead to the center. And at the center… awaits the Minotaur."

"Then I'll burn the maze down," Lyra said, her eyes flashing with a spark of her true defiance.

Lorcan's eyes widened almost imperceptibly, a flicker of something akin to surprise, quickly masked. A genuine smile, more pronounced than before, finally graced his lips. "A fascinating response. Most would try to find the exit. Or scream." He leaned back, his gaze thoughtful. "You are not an easy puzzle to solve, Lyra Virellan."

He picked up a small, exquisitely carved wooden box from a nearby table. He ran his thumb over its smooth surface, his gaze distant. "Let us try a different path then. Tell me a truth about yourself that no one else knows. A truth that would surprise even Cassian."

Lyra's mind raced. This was a trap. Any real truth could be used against her. She needed to give him something, but nothing that would compromise her mission.

"I secretly enjoy bad puns," she said, her voice completely serious. "The groan-worthy kind. The worse, the better."

Lorcan paused, the hand holding the box stilling. He stared at her, his deep eyes searching for any hint of deception. Then, a slow, disbelieving laugh bubbled up from his chest. It was a quieter, more intellectual sound than Cassian's boisterous amusement, but no less genuine.

"A preference for… terrible wordplay?" he repeated, shaking his head. "After all that talk of burning mazes? You disappoint me, Lyra." His eyes twinkled. "Or perhaps… you simply know how to deflect."

"A little bit of both, perhaps," Lyra admitted, a small, knowing smile on her own lips.

He placed the wooden box back down, his gaze softening almost imperceptibly. "You are clever, Lyra Virellan. Dangerously so." He leaned forward again, his voice dropping once more, now devoid of any playfulness, becoming grave. "But cleverness alone will not save you in this place. Be wary of gifts, Lyra. Especially those that glitter. And be wary of shadows. For the deepest manipulations are often born in the dark."

His words hung in the air, a chilling warning. Lyra felt a cold dread settle in her stomach. This wasn't just a philosophical game for Lorcan. He knew something. He was hinting at a deeper conspiracy, a larger game at play within the castle walls. Vampire politics. It had already begun.

Just then, Cassian reappeared, his golden eyes sweeping over them, assessing the silent tableau. "Has the puzzle been solved, brother?" he asked, a possessive edge to his voice as he looked at Lyra.

Lorcan looked from Lyra to Cassian, a complex expression on his face – resignation mixed with something akin to concern. "The puzzle remains… open, Cassian," he said. "But the pieces are certainly intriguing." His gaze returned to Lyra, holding hers for a moment, a silent message passing between them. "She is not what she seems."

Cassian's lips curved into a slow, confident smile. "I never expected her to be." He extended his hand to Lyra. "Come, Lyra. The night is young. And I have further… plans for you."

Lyra rose, meeting Cassian's gaze. The air around him still hummed with dangerous desire, but Lorcan's quiet warning resonated in her ears. She had gained a tiny bit of insight, a fragment of the larger picture. She had also confirmed that Cassian was a complex, unpredictable adversary, and Lorcan, a subtle, potentially sympathetic informant.

As she allowed Cassian to guide her away, back into the swirling opulence of the ballroom, Lyra knew one thing for certain. The game had just become infinitely more complicated. And the lies, like the ancient stones of Sinful Castle, ran deeper than she could ever have imagined.

Chapter 5: Silk and Steel

The night at Sinful Castle stretched on, an intoxicating blend of power, opulence, and veiled menace. Lyra remained at Cassian's side for much of the "gathering," a silent trophy, a bold statement. He introduced her to a few other high-ranking vampires, his hand often resting on her back or arm, a constant reminder of his claim. Each introduction was a subtle performance, Lyra playing the role of the intriguing, slightly defiant mortal, while Cassian exuded possessive pride. She observed the various factions, the subtle nods of alliance, the sharp glares of rivalry. The political landscape of the vampire court was as intricate and deadly as any mortal one.

Lorcan remained on the periphery, his deep eyes often finding hers across the crowded room, a silent, watchful presence. His earlier warning echoed in her mind: "Be wary of gifts... and be wary of shadows." She didn't know what he meant, but the words settled like a cold stone in her stomach.

As the gathering began to wind down, Cassian led Lyra away from the main ballroom, through another series of opulent corridors, this time leading to a more private wing of the castle. The air here was thicker, richer, scented with something ancient and potent. This was clearly the inner sanctum.

They stopped before a set of double doors, carved from dark, polished wood, inlaid with intricate silver designs that shimmered faintly in the dim light. Cassian pushed them open with a single, fluid motion, revealing a chamber that made Lyra's breath hitch.

This was clearly Cassian's private domain. The room was immense, luxurious, and undeniably masculine. A vast, four-poster bed, draped in crimson velvet, dominated one end, its posts carved into the likeness of snarling gargoyles. A massive fireplace roared with white-hot flames, casting flickering shadows across the walls, which were lined with shelves of ancient tomes and a formidable collection of gleaming, ornate weapons – swords, daggers, axes, each one a work of art and a tool of death.

The air thrummed with his presence, thick with his unique scent, a blend of blood, power, and something darkly alluring. This was the predator's lair.

"Welcome," Cassian murmured, his voice a low, resonant purr that seemed to vibrate through the very floor. "To my chambers." He didn't enter immediately, allowing her to take in the surroundings, to feel the weight of his power in this space.

Lyra walked in, her gaze sweeping over the room, cataloging every detail, every potential threat, every possible escape route – though she knew those were likely non-existent. She could feel his golden eyes on her, watching her reaction. She kept her face impassive.

"Impressive," she stated, her voice devoid of emotion, though internally, she was assessing the sheer scale of his power, evident in every detail of the room.

He chuckled, a low, satisfied sound. "I aim to please." He finally stepped into the room, closing the doors behind him with a soft click that resonated like a finality. He walked towards a large, intricately carved chest at the foot of his bed. "However," he continued, his voice taking on a different tone, one of anticipation, "tonight's preparations are not quite complete."

He opened the chest, and Lyra's eyes widened almost imperceptibly. Inside, nestled on crimson silk, was a single gown.

It was a dress of sheer, almost translucent black silk, so fine it seemed to float on air. It was cut in a way that would cling to every curve, revealing rather than concealing. Long, flowing sleeves of the same delicate fabric trailed to the floor, and the neckline plunged daringly. It was a gown designed not just to be beautiful, but to provoke. To tempt. To strip away all pretense.

"This," Cassian said, his voice a silken whisper, "is for the first selection night. For *our* first selection night." His golden eyes met hers, burning with an intense, possessive heat. "I believe it will suit you… perfectly."

Lyra stared at the dress, then at him. The message was clear. This wasn't a choice; it was a command. He wanted her utterly exposed, vulnerable, on display for him. It was an act of complete dominance, a psychological game as much as a physical one.

I came here to kill people. Not to do a bloody fashion lookbook. The thought, this time, was a desperate attempt to cling to her sanity, to the purpose that had brought her here.

The sheer audacity of his expectation, to have her dress up for her own "consumption," was infuriating.

"You expect me to wear that?" she asked, her voice dangerously calm, a razor's edge beneath the surface.

Cassian's lips curved into a slow, confident smile. "I expect you to. Unless, of course, you prefer to remain… unadorned." His eyes dropped to her current, simple gray dress, then back to her face, a clear challenge.

A battle of wills ignited in the air between them. Lyra felt the heat rise in her cheeks, a mix of anger and a strange, unwelcome awareness of the raw desire in his gaze. He wanted her to react. He wanted her to resist, so he could break her.

But Lyra had learned long ago that the fastest way to truly defeat an opponent was to play their game, then turn it on its head. She would not give him the satisfaction of seeing her outrage, or her fear.

She let out a soft, almost imperceptible sigh, a theatrical gesture of mock resignation. "Fine," she said, her voice surprisingly light, almost bored. "If I must. But you're paying for the dry cleaning."

Cassian blinked. The confident smirk faltered for a fraction of a second, replaced by a flicker of genuine surprise. He hadn't expected that. He'd expected defiance, or tears, or a dramatic refusal. Not… dry cleaning.

Then, a low, rumbling chuckle started in his chest, growing into a full, rich laugh, much like the one she'd provoked in the antechamber. He threw his head back, his eyes gleaming with delight. "Dry cleaning," he repeated, still laughing. "You truly are... a marvel, Lyra Virellan."

He took a step closer, his golden eyes still dancing with amusement. "I assure you, little mortal, cost is no object here. And besides," he leaned in, his voice dropping to a seductive whisper, his gaze trailing over her, "I doubt it will stay clean for long."

Lyra met his gaze, her own eyes holding a cool, defiant glint. "We'll see about that," she murmured, a silent promise. She would wear his dress, yes. But it wouldn't be for his pleasure alone. It would be her armor, her disguise. The silk might be sheer, but her will was steel.

She walked towards the chest, her movements deliberate, unhurried. She picked up the dress, the impossibly soft fabric feeling like a whisper against her fingertips. It was beautiful, dangerous, and utterly revealing.

This isn't about being seen, she thought, a cold resolve settling in her heart. *This is about seeing them.*

She turned to Cassian, a small, enigmatic smile playing on her lips. "If you'll excuse me, Lord Cassian," she said, her voice dripping with mock politeness. "I believe I have a wardrobe change to attend to. Unless, of course, you intend to... assist?"

His golden eyes blazed, a potent mix of desire and amusement. "The thought is certainly tempting," he purred, taking a step closer. "But I prefer to savor the reveal. Take your time, little mortal. I shall be waiting."

He gestured towards a door she hadn't noticed before, subtly hidden in a shadowed corner of the room. A dressing chamber, no doubt. Lyra nodded, then walked towards it, the sheer black silk a dark whisper in her hands.

As the door closed softly behind her, Lyra held the dress up, examining its provocative design. *If I'm going to be an offering,* she thought, her lips curving into a grim, determined smile, *I'll be the one they never forget. The one who brought the house down, in silk and steel.*

The first selection night. The dance of the predator and prey. Lyra knew it was just beginning. And she was ready to make her move.

Chapter 6: The Dance Begins

The sheer black silk dress was a second skin, clinging to Lyra's form with an almost indecent intimacy. It offered no concealment, no comfort, just a stark, undeniable statement of vulnerability. Yet, as Lyra stood before the full-length mirror in Cassian's dressing chamber, she saw not weakness, but a sharpened blade. The fabric might be translucent, but her resolve was as opaque as the deepest night. The small, concealed dagger rested cool against her inner thigh, a promise of retribution beneath the deceptive allure.

She ran a hand over the silk, a ghost of a smile touching her lips. *If I'm going down, I'm going fabulous.* The thought, a dark jest to herself, brought a flicker of grim satisfaction. This was her stage, her performance. And she intended to leave a lasting impression.

A soft knock on the dressing chamber door announced Cassian's presence. "Ready, little mortal?" His voice, a low rumble, held an undeniable note of anticipation.

Lyra took a deep breath, pushing down the surge of unease that always accompanied his proximity. "As I'll ever be, Lord Cassian," she called back, her voice clear and steady.

She opened the door, stepping out into his opulent bedchamber. Cassian was waiting, standing by the roaring fireplace, his form silhouetted against the dancing flames. He had changed into an even more elaborate suit of dark velvet, subtly embroidered with silver thread that gleamed in the firelight. He looked every inch the lord of this dark domain, a creature of lethal elegance.

His golden eyes swept over her, taking in the full effect of the dress. A slow, appreciative smile spread across his lips, and his eyes darkened with a raw, undeniable hunger that made Lyra's breath catch. It wasn't just physical desire; it was a predatory possessiveness that radiated from him like heat.

"Exquisite," he murmured, his voice husky. He took a step closer, his gaze lingering on the curve of her throat, the delicate line of her collarbone revealed by the sheer fabric. "Truly exquisite."

He extended his hand, his long, elegant fingers reaching for hers. Lyra hesitated for a fraction of a second, then placed her hand in his. His skin was cool, smooth, and his grip firm, almost possessive. It wasn't a gentle invitation; it was a claim.

"Come," he said, his voice a low command. "The true dance begins now."

He led her out of his chambers and down another series of corridors, grander and more brightly lit than before. They led to a massive, circular hall Lyra hadn't seen yet. This was not the ballroom from earlier; this was a dedicated space, designed for… something more intimate, more intense.

The hall was filled with fewer vampires than before, perhaps fifty or sixty at most, all of whom were clearly high-ranking members of Cassian's court. They were arranged around the perimeter of a vast, polished marble floor, their faces a mixture of curious anticipation and veiled resentment. Soft, haunting music played from an unseen source, a melancholic waltz that seemed to pull at the very air.

At the center of the hall, two other "offerings" were already dancing with vampires. One girl, her face pale with terror, was being led in a stiff, uncomfortable waltz by an older, more sinister-looking vampire whose eyes never left her throat. The other, a defiant redhead, struggled against the elegant but firm grip of her partner, her eyes flashing with impotent rage.

This was the "first selection night" Cassian had spoken of. Not a social gathering, but a ritualistic display, a public claiming, and perhaps, a test of submission.

As Cassian led Lyra onto the polished floor, every eye in the room turned to them. A ripple went through the assembled vampires, a low hum of curiosity and assessment. Lyra felt the weight of their gazes, a tangible pressure on her skin. She kept her posture regal, her expression neutral. She would not give them the satisfaction of seeing her fear.

Cassian positioned her, his hand moving to the small of her back, his fingers spread wide, burning through the thin silk. His other hand took hers, lacing their fingers together. He was close, too close, his tall frame towering over her. She could feel the heat emanating from his body, the subtle hum of his immense power.

The music swelled, and he began to lead. He was an excellent dancer, his movements fluid, powerful, utterly dominant. He didn't ask her to follow; he simply moved, and Lyra, with years of training in various forms of movement and combat, instinctively kept pace. She allowed him to guide her, matching his steps, spinning when he spun, her body moving in sync with his, a dangerous intimacy that belied the tension thrumming between them.

He pulled her closer, their bodies almost brushing, the sheer silk of her dress a flimsy barrier. His head dipped, his lips almost touching her ear. "You dance well, Lyra Virellan," he murmured, his voice a low, possessive growl. "Better than the others."

"I learn quickly," she replied, her voice calm, though her heart hammered a frantic rhythm against her ribs. She could feel the subtle shift in his weight, the powerful muscles of his back flexing beneath her hand.

His grip on her waist tightened, pulling her flush against his solid form. Lyra felt the unmistakable pressure of his body against hers, the undeniable strength of him. Her senses were overwhelmed by his presence, by the rich, metallic scent of him that was now dangerously close.

He inhaled deeply, his nose brushing against her hair, then tracing the delicate line of her jaw, moving closer to her neck. Lyra felt a shiver, an almost primal response, as his cold breath ghosted over her pulse point. This was it. The moment she had anticipated, dreaded, and prepared for. The first true hint of his monstrous nature, his insatiable hunger.

"Your blood," he whispered, his voice dark with desire, his fangs, she knew, elongated and poised, inches from her skin. "It sings to me. A song of… defiance. And something else." He inhaled again, deeper this time, his lips brushing lightly against her skin, a feather-light touch that promised agonizing pleasure. "Something sweet. Something intoxicating."

Lyra felt her pulse quicken, not from fear, but from a strange, dangerous excitement. The air crackled with tension, so thick she could almost taste it. Every instinct screamed at her to pull away, to fight, to scream. But she held firm, her body a rigid line against his. She would not break. Not here. Not now.

His lips were on her neck, a soft, probing touch. Lyra felt a surge of adrenaline, her muscles tensing, ready to react. This was the moment. The very edge of the precipice.

Then, just as his fangs were about to pierce her skin, he pulled back. Only an inch, but it was enough to break the spell. He straightened, his golden eyes blazing down at her, filled with a potent mix of frustrated hunger and… something else. Admiration? Challenge?

"You surprise me, Lyra Virellan," he murmured, his voice now a low, dangerous growl. "You do not tremble. You do not beg."

Lyra met his gaze, her heart still pounding, but her voice steady. "Why should I?" she challenged, a subtle, almost imperceptible smirk touching her lips. "A good meal should be savored, not rushed."

Cassian stared at her for a long moment, a complex array of emotions warring in his golden eyes. Frustration, desire, a flicker of genuine amusement, and something Lyra couldn't quite decipher. He was intrigued. He was challenged. And he clearly enjoyed it.

He let out a low, guttural sound, not quite a growl, not quite a laugh, but something in between. His hand on her waist tightened to an almost painful degree, asserting his dominance, his possessive claim.

"Indeed," he finally said, his voice laced with dark promise. "And I intend to savor every single moment of you, Lyra Virellan. Every drop."

He spun her, the movement fluid and powerful, bringing her into a deeper embrace, pulling her even closer. The dance continued, a silent battle of wills, a dangerous flirtation with destiny. Lyra, pressed intimately against the formidable body of her captor, knew that the game was just beginning. And the stakes had just been raised infinitely higher. The first bite had almost happened, a prelude to a deeper, more complex claim than simple hunger.

Chapter 7: Blood and Banter

The waltz continued, a relentless spiral of power and desire. Cassian held Lyra impossibly close, his body a solid wall against hers, his golden eyes burning into her own. Each turn, each dip, was a subtle assertion of his dominance, a test of her composure. The sheer silk of her dress offered no protection, only a heightened awareness of every point of contact.

The other vampires watched, their expressions a mix of hunger, envy, and a chilling fascination. They weren't merely observing a dance; they were witnessing a delicate, dangerous game of cat and mouse, and they were eager to see who would break first.

Lyra, however, refused to yield. She met his intensity with her own, her eyes holding a cool, unyielding defiance. She followed his lead, not out of submission, but with the precise, calculated movements of a dancer who knew every step, even in a waltz with the devil himself.

As they spun near the edge of the polished floor, the music swelling to a crescendo, Cassian dipped her low, her back arching precariously. His lips brushed against her neck again, a hair's breadth from her pulse. "Still not afraid, little mortal?" he murmured, his voice a husky growl, a direct challenge.

Lyra's breath hitched, but she held his gaze, her lips curving into a faint, almost imperceptible smirk. "Should I be?" she whispered, her voice surprisingly steady, a mere breath against his ear. "I thought vampires enjoyed a challenge. Or do you prefer your meals to be... pre-tenderized?"

A low growl rumbled in Cassian's chest, a sound that would have sent most mortals scrambling. But a flicker of something else, something akin to surprise, crossed his features. He straightened, pulling her back up, their bodies still intimately pressed together. His golden eyes narrowed, a potent mix of frustration and intrigue.

"You push your luck," he stated, his voice devoid of humor.

"And you savor the game," Lyra countered, her gaze unwavering. "Otherwise, you would have bitten me already."

He leaned in again, his breath warm against her ear, the metallic scent of him intoxicatingly close. "Don't tempt me, Lyra Virellan," he purred, his voice raw with a barely restrained hunger. "My patience, though ancient, is not infinite."

"Patience is a virtue, Lord Cassian," Lyra retorted, her voice light, almost mocking. "And virtues, I hear, are in short supply among your kind."

A beat of silence. Then, a low, guttural chuckle escaped him, a genuine, surprised sound that reverberated through her. It wasn't the amused huff from before; this was a deeper, more visceral laugh, born of sheer disbelief and a grudging admiration. He actually threw his head back, a flash of pure, unadulterated amusement lighting his golden eyes.

"You," he said, shaking his head slightly, still chuckling, "are utterly insufferable."

"And you, Lord Cassian," Lyra replied, her smile widening into a genuine, mischievous grin, "are surprisingly easy to rile."

The laughter died down, replaced by a lingering, almost dangerous glint in his eyes. He stopped dancing, though he didn't release her. They stood in the middle of the polished floor, a silent, intimate tableau, the music a distant hum around them. The other vampires, sensing the shift in dynamics, had largely averted their gazes, giving them a wide berth.

"You amuse me," Cassian stated, his voice low, almost a confession. "Too much, perhaps." His thumb traced the line of her jaw, then brushed lightly over her lower lip, his gaze fixed on her mouth. "That could be… dangerous for you."

"And for you," Lyra countered softly, her gaze holding his. "Predictability is safe. I am anything but."

His eyes darkened, his expression turning serious. "Indeed. And danger, little mortal, is precisely what draws the hunter."

He pulled her even closer, so close that their chests brushed with every breath. Lyra could feel the powerful beat of his immortal heart, a slow, steady thrum against her own frantic rhythm.

"Tell me," he whispered, his voice deep and resonant, "what is it you truly want, Lyra Virellan? Beyond this… charade?"

It was a probing question, aimed at the core of her being. Lyra knew she couldn't reveal her true purpose. She needed a deflection, a truth mixed with enough wit to keep him intrigued, but not enough to expose her.

"I want control," she said, her voice dropping to a low, almost husky murmur. "To choose my own fate. To be… unbound." She met his gaze, letting her eyes convey a fierce, unyielding independence. "If I kneel, it'll be to trip you, not to worship you."

Cassian's eyes widened, a flash of something intense – shock? admiration? – in their depths. He stared at her, utterly still, for a long moment. Then, a ghost of a smile touched his lips, a slow, dangerous curve.

"Unbound," he repeated, the word a soft caress on his tongue. "A challenging desire." He leaned in, his mouth hovering just above hers, his breath mingling with hers. "But perhaps… some bonds are meant to be forged, not broken. Bonds of… exquisite control."

His golden eyes held hers, a silent promise of a different kind of captivity, one laced with undeniable desire. The air crackled with the unspent energy between them. Lyra felt a peculiar tension – a dread mixed with a potent, almost forbidden curiosity. She was walking a tightrope, balancing defiance with a dangerous allure.

He slowly, deliberately, released her, taking a step back. The sudden absence of his heat, his presence, left an inexplicable chill in the air.

"The night is still young, Lyra Virellan," he said, his voice returning to its normal, commanding tone, though a lingering huskiness remained. "And there are many more lessons to be learned." He gestured towards the tables laden with food and drink. "Perhaps you would care for a refreshment? Though I suspect… you have a different kind of thirst."

Lyra's lips curled into a faint, knowing smile. "Always, Lord Cassian. Always." She met his gaze, a silent challenge in her eyes. "But I prefer to choose my own vintage."

He watched her, a low, appreciative hum escaping him. The chemistry between them was undeniable, a dangerous, thrilling current that ran beneath their words. Lyra knew she was pushing boundaries, but the more she pushed, the more intrigued he became. And intrigue, she realized, was a powerful weapon.

She walked towards one of the tables, a subtle sway in her step, the black silk whispering around her. She felt his gaze on her back, a tangible weight. She had surprised him. She had amused him. And she had, perhaps, just earned herself a little more time, a little more leverage, in the deadly game she had willingly entered. The banter was just another layer of the seduction, a dance of wits as dangerous as any physical confrontation.

Chapter 8: Test of Pain, Taste of Power

The atmosphere in the grand hall shifted as the night deepened. The initial air of celebration began to thin, replaced by a palpable tension. Lyra, lingering near the refreshment tables, observed the other offerings. Their initial composure was fraying, replaced by a nervous energy. The older vampires, those who had chosen their "partners" for the night, now moved with a more focused intensity, their gazes lingering on the throats of their chosen mortals.

Cassian reappeared by Lyra's side, seemingly out of nowhere. His presence was a familiar weight now, a dangerous hum beneath the surface of the night. "Enjoying your vintage?" he murmured, his golden eyes sweeping over her, a possessive gleam in their depths.

"Adequately," Lyra replied, her voice cool. She had merely taken a sip of a blood-red liquid that was, mercifully, just wine. She didn't want to dull her senses.

He chuckled, a low, appreciative sound. "I expected nothing less. You are... particular." He inclined his head towards the center of the hall, where a small group of vampires had gathered, a few of the offerings among them. "The next phase of the selection is about to begin."

Lyra felt a prickle of anticipation. This was it. The real test. The "elimination." She had learned enough of these rituals to know they were rarely gentle.

A vampire, ancient and severe, with a face like carved granite, stepped forward. He was one of the High Lords, she recognized, though not Arkyn. His voice, raspy and cold, cut through the murmuring crowd. "Brothers and sisters of the blood! Tonight, we welcome new life into our fold, new vessels to sate the ancient Thirst. But not all are worthy. Not all possess the fortitude. The weak shall be culled. The resilient… shall be embraced."

A collective gasp went through the remaining offerings. Lyra's eyes narrowed. *Culled.* A euphemism for death, or something worse.

The High Lord gestured to a young woman, perhaps nineteen or twenty, with wide, terrified eyes. She was one of the "chosen" from earlier, paired with the ice-eyed vampire. "Melina," the High Lord intoned. "You have been chosen by Lord Valerius." Lord Valerius, a vampire of chilling composure, stepped forward, his gaze fixed on the girl.

"The test of fortitude," the High Lord continued, his voice echoing in the chamber, "is simple. Endure the First Touch. Endure the Thirst. Without fear. Without weakness. For only then can true communion begin."

Lyra watched, her senses on high alert. This wasn't a public feeding. This was a ritualized "first bite," designed to assess the mortal's reaction, to gauge their spirit.

Lord Valerius approached Melina. His movements were slow, deliberate, drawing out the terror. Melina began to tremble, her pale face slick with sweat, her eyes darting frantically around the room, pleading.

"No," she whimpered, a raw, desperate sound that pierced the opulent silence. "Please… no!"

Lord Valerius paid her no mind. He reached out, his hand grasping her chin, tilting her head back, exposing the delicate curve of her throat. His fangs, long and gleaming, descended slowly, inexorably, towards her skin.

Melina's whimper turned into a choked sob, then a full-blown scream as his fangs pierced her. It was a visceral, horrifying sound that tore through the festive air, echoing off the high ceilings. Her body convulsed, a desperate, pathetic struggle against an impossible strength.

The bite lasted only a few agonizing seconds. Lord Valerius pulled back, his lips stained crimson, his eyes momentarily gleaming with satiated hunger. Melina collapsed, her body twitching, a small, dark stain spreading on the silk of her dress. Her eyes were still wide, but now they were glazed, empty. She was alive, but something vital had gone out of her.

"Weakness," the High Lord declared, his voice devoid of pity. "Her spirit is broken. She is... no longer suitable."

Two silent, cloaked guards moved forward instantly, lifting Melina's limp form from the floor. She was carried away, her fate sealed. Lyra felt a chill run down her spine, not from fear for herself, but from the chilling display of cold, merciless power. Melina hadn't been killed outright, but her soul had been devoured.

Lyra glanced at Cassian. His expression was unreadable, his golden eyes fixed on the retreating form of Melina. There was no pity in his gaze, no sympathy. Only a cold, detached assessment. This was their reality. This was their world.

"Such a waste," Lyra murmured, her voice just loud enough for him to hear.

Cassian turned his head, his golden eyes fixing on her. "A waste of potential," he agreed, his voice flat. "Fear makes the blood sour. It makes the spirit... brittle." He took a step closer, his gaze intense. "You, little mortal, possess no such brittleness."

Lyra met his gaze without flinching. "I prefer to break the mold, not be broken by it."

A faint, almost imperceptible smirk touched his lips. "Indeed." He paused, then inclined his head towards the High Lord. "Your turn approaches, Lyra Virellan."

Lyra's heart hammered against her ribs. This was it. Her "vết cắn kiểm định" (test bite). The moment of true vulnerability, when her carefully constructed facade might crack.

The High Lord called her name. "Lyra Virellan. Chosen by Lord Cassian."

All eyes in the hall turned to her. Lyra felt the weight of their combined anticipation, their hunger, their judgment. She walked towards the center of the hall, her movements graceful, deliberate. She didn't look at Cassian. She focused on the cold marble beneath her feet, on the steady rhythm of her own breathing.

She stopped before the High Lord. Cassian moved, positioning himself directly behind her, his presence a wall of power at her back. His hand rested lightly on her waist, a familiar, possessive touch that sent a strange warmth through her.

The High Lord began the ritualistic incantation, his voice droning, a prelude to the inevitable. Lyra closed her eyes for a fleeting second, centering herself. *This is not surrender. This is information. This is a weapon.*

She opened her eyes, meeting the High Lord's cold gaze. He looked past her, towards Cassian. "Lord Cassian, you may claim your First Touch. Taste her spirit."

Cassian's breath ghosted over her ear, his voice a low, intimate whisper that sent shivers down her spine. "Ready, little mortal?"

Lyra said nothing. She simply tilted her head, exposing the sensitive skin of her neck, a gesture of mock compliance. Her pulse throbbed, a rapid beat against her skin.

She felt the cold brush of his lips, feather-light, exploring the delicate skin. Then, the sharp, exquisite pain as his fangs pierced her. It was a sudden, intense sting, followed by a burning sensation that spread rapidly through her veins. But it wasn't just pain. Beneath the pain, a strange, dizzying wave of euphoria began to bloom, a forbidden pleasure that shocked her to her core.

She gasped, a soft, involuntary sound. Her hands instinctively curled into fists, but she didn't struggle. She focused on the sensation, on the warmth spreading from the bite, on the curious lightness in her head. It was half pain, half pleasure, a bewildering dichotomy that left her momentarily breathless.

She could feel the subtle suction as he drew her blood, a steady, rhythmic pull. Her vision blurred at the edges, and the world seemed to tilt. The music in the hall seemed to fade, replaced by the rushing sound of her own blood, the primal rhythm of Cassian's feeding. It was intimate, invasive, and terrifyingly... addictive.

He pulled back, slowly, his fangs disengaging with a soft, wet sound. Lyra felt a dizzying emptiness, a faint tremor running through her limbs. He lingered for a moment, his lips still brushing her skin, then finally straightened.

Lyra swayed slightly, her hand instinctively going to her neck, where a small, blooming warmth throbbed. She felt lightheaded, disoriented, but strangely... invigorated. And then, a wave of defiant amusement washed over her.

She looked up at Cassian, her eyes still a little unfocused, but with a spark of mischievous defiance. His golden eyes, now dark and sated, stared back at her, a hint of surprise in their depths.

"Well," Lyra managed, a faint, almost breathless laugh escaping her lips, "that was... memorable." She touched the small, bleeding mark on her neck. "We should put a napkin next time, Lord Cassian. You're a messy eater."

A stunned silence fell over the hall. The vampires who had been watching, expecting screams, tears, or a broken spirit, stared in disbelief. Cassian himself froze, his golden eyes widening, a rare look of genuine astonishment on his face. He blinked, then looked from the High Lord, to the confused audience, and finally back to Lyra, who was now grinning faintly despite the throbbing pain in her neck.

Then, a low, rumbling laugh escaped Cassian, a sound of sheer, unadulterated delight that filled the hall. It was louder, more robust than any he had produced before. He threw his head back, shaking with silent mirth.

"Remarkable," he finally gasped, still chuckling, his eyes bright with a dangerous amusement. "Truly, Lyra Virellan, you are… utterly remarkable." He looked at the High Lord, a predatory smile on his lips. "She is clearly… suitable. More than suitable."

The High Lord, still slightly stunned, could only nod mutely.

Cassian turned back to Lyra, his hand finding hers, his grip warm and possessive. "Come, little mortal," he murmured, his gaze sweeping over her face, a possessive satisfaction in his eyes. "The night is still young. And I have many more lessons to teach you."

Lyra walked with him, a strange mix of triumph and bewilderment swirling within her. She had survived the test. She had not only endured the bite, but had shocked her captor, and perhaps, even impressed him. The pain was still there, but so was the intoxicating echo of pleasure, and the exhilarating taste of a small victory. The game had just begun a new, more dangerous phase.

Chapter 9: The Monster Beneath the Mask

The "test bite" had left Lyra feeling strangely invigorated, a peculiar mix of lingering pain, a faint, heady rush, and a defiant triumph. The other offerings now looked at her with a blend of awe and fear, and even some of the older vampires regarded her with a new, grudging respect. She had faced the beast and not only survived but had made it laugh.

Cassian, his golden eyes still alight with a dangerous amusement, led her away from the stunned assembly. He guided her through a series of grand arches and into a more secluded part of the hall, where plush, velvet-covered seating awaited. The music here was softer, more melancholic, a haunting cello melody that seemed to speak of ancient sorrows.

He settled into a large armchair, gesturing for Lyra to take the smaller one opposite him. Lyra sat, her hand instinctively going to her neck, where the small bite mark pulsed with a dull ache. She could still feel the phantom touch of his fangs, the strange, dizzying pleasure that had mixed with the pain. It was unsettling, this new sensation, this unexpected response her body had to the very thing she detested.

Cassian watched her, his gaze intense, assessing. "Does it displease you, little mortal?" he asked, his voice low, almost gentle, a stark contrast to his earlier predatory growl.

Lyra looked at him, her eyes steady. "It is… an experience," she conceded, choosing her words carefully. "Unpleasant, yet… informative."

He let out a soft, almost inaudible chuckle. "Informative. Always seeking knowledge, are we?" He leaned forward, his elbows resting on his knees, his posture unexpectedly relaxed, almost human. "Tell me, what did you learn?"

"That your kind are… messy eaters," Lyra retorted, a faint smile touching her lips. The banter was a shield, a way to maintain control in a situation where she had very little.

Cassian's lips curved into a genuine smile, a flash of white fangs. "A valid observation." He paused, then his expression shifted, a subtle darkening in his golden eyes. "And what else?"

Lyra's gaze met his. "That power has many tastes," she said, her voice dropping to a more serious tone. "And that some appetites are never truly sated."

His smile faded, replaced by a thoughtful, almost distant look. He picked up a goblet of dark liquid from a nearby table – freshly drawn blood, Lyra presumed. He took a slow sip, his gaze drifting away, across the room, towards nothing in particular. He seemed to be lost in thought, his formidable presence momentarily softened, more vulnerable.

It was in this moment of quiet contemplation that Lyra noticed it. A faint, almost imperceptible scar, a thin white line running just beneath his left jawline, disappearing under his collar. It was old, almost faded, hidden by the perfect angles of his face, but now, in the soft, flickering light, it was visible. A wound. A scar on a creature supposedly immortal, untouchable.

Her eyes widened slightly. *He has been hurt.* It was a revelation, a crack in the monstrous façade he so carefully cultivated. She had always imagined them as invincible, pristine, devoid of imperfection. But this tiny mark told a different story. A story of pain. A story of a past.

Cassian, sensing her prolonged gaze, turned his head, his golden eyes meeting hers. He saw her looking at the scar. For a fleeting second, a shadow crossed his face, a raw, almost human expression of... something akin to discomfort, or perhaps, a flash of memory. It was quickly masked, but Lyra had seen it. The monster had a wound.

"Curious, little mortal?" he asked, his voice now colder, a hint of steel returning to it.

Lyra didn't flinch. "I observe," she stated, her voice calm. "Like you."

His gaze sharpened, but he didn't immediately turn away. Instead, he reached up, his long fingers lightly tracing the scar on his own jaw. His expression was unreadable, a wall had descended.

"Some scars," he murmured, his voice a low, almost husky whisper, "are deeper than blood. They are... carved into the very bone." He took another slow sip of his drink, his eyes distant, as if reliving a memory. "They serve as… reminders."

"Of what?" Lyra pressed softly, a rare moment of genuine curiosity overriding her caution.

He looked at her then, his golden eyes filled with an ancient weariness that seemed to contradict his powerful youthfulness. "Of the price of power," he said, his voice laced with a subtle bitterness. "And the price of… devotion. Even from those who betray you."

His words were enigmatic, laden with unspoken history. Lyra felt a chill, not from the cold of the castle, but from the raw emotion she glimpsed beneath his carefully constructed mask of control. This was not just a vampire; this was a being with a past, with wounds, with betrayals. It made him more complex, more dangerous, and, unnervingly, more… human.

"Everyone has scars, Lord Cassian," Lyra said quietly, her voice surprisingly empathetic. "Some are just harder to see." She thought of her own, invisible wounds, carved by grief and the burning desire for vengeance.

He regarded her for a long moment, his golden eyes searching, probing. He seemed to see past her defiance, past her wit, to something deeper within her. "Indeed," he finally conceded, his voice softer than she had ever heard it. "And some are… shared. Even across species."

He finished his drink, setting the goblet down with a soft clink. The brief moment of vulnerability, of shared understanding, seemed to dissipate like mist. The powerful, predatory aura returned, cloaking him once more.

"Enough introspection," he said, his voice regaining its usual commanding tone. "The night still holds... opportunities. And you, little mortal, are my current fascination." He rose from his chair, his movements fluid and powerful once more.

Lyra rose too, her senses alert. The brief glimpse of his vulnerability, of the "monster beneath the mask," had revealed a new layer to her formidable captor. He wasn't just a brutal beast; he was a scarred survivor, driven by complex motivations. And that made him infinitely more dangerous, and perhaps, a potential key to understanding the true enemy.

As he turned to lead her deeper into the castle, Lyra's mind whirred. The joke about dental insurance, a fleeting thought during their initial encounter, now seemed to hold a darker irony. *Nice fangs. Ever considered dental insurance?* No, she thought, a grim smile touching her lips. Clearly, he hadn't. And the price of that oversight was a scar, a wound that told a story she desperately needed to uncover.

The revelations, small as they were, were piling up. The game was no longer just about survival and vengeance. It was about unraveling a complex tapestry of secrets, betrayals, and ancient power. And Lyra, the human girl caught in the center of it all, found herself drawn deeper into the dark, alluring mystery of the vampire who had marked her.

Chapter 10: Secrets Written in Bone

The night had finally begun to wane, the first faint whispers of dawn threatening to pierce the eternal twilight of Sinful Castle. Cassian, having grown restless after their brief, unsettling moment of shared vulnerability, had rejoined a circle of his peers, leaving Lyra momentarily to her own devices. This was the opening she had been waiting for.

Her "test bite" and the subsequent unexpected banter had granted her a degree of freedom, a fleeting moment where the ever-present vampire eyes were less vigilant, perhaps lulled by her performance. Now was the time to act. Lorcan's warning echoed in her mind: *"Be wary of shadows. For the deepest manipulations are often born in the dark."* He had hinted at a larger game, a hidden agenda. And Lorcan, the quiet observer, was the most likely to keep records.

Lyra moved with purpose, blending into the thinning crowd. Her black silk dress, once a symbol of her intended humiliation, now served as excellent camouflage in the castle's shadowy corridors. The throbbing ache in her neck was a constant reminder of Cassian's bite, a strangely invigorating sensation that kept her senses sharp.

She remembered the way Lorcan had subtly gestured towards a particular wing of the castle earlier in the night, a fleeting glance that could have been dismissed as accidental. But Lyra had trained herself to notice such things. She followed her instincts, navigating the labyrinthine passages with a blend of memory and intuition, guided by the faint scent of ancient parchment and something cool, almost metallic – the lingering aura of powerful magic.

The corridors grew quieter, less opulent, giving way to narrower, colder passages. The tapestries became older, more worn, depicting esoteric symbols Lyra didn't recognize but instinctively understood were significant. This felt like the older, less frequented parts of the castle, a place where secrets might genuinely reside.

She found it: a heavy, unadorned wooden door, almost indistinguishable from the stone wall, marked only by a faint, almost invisible symbol carved into its surface – a stylized eye, half-closed. It was Lorcan's crest, she realized, recalling a fleeting glimpse of a ring on his finger earlier.

The door was locked, of course. But Lyra had anticipated this. Years of covert training had equipped her with more than just a blade. She produced a set of finely crafted lock-picks from a hidden pocket in her dress, a miracle of concealment for a garment so sheer. Her fingers, nimble and precise, danced over the tumblers, listening to the soft clicks and scrapes within. It took a few tense moments, but then, with a soft thunk, the lock gave way.

Lyra slipped inside, closing the door silently behind her. The room was dark, but a faint, silvery light emanated from a large, circular window high on one wall, casting ethereal patterns on the floor. It was a study, vast and filled with the scent of aged paper, ink, and a subtle, scholarly vampire essence.

Shelves upon shelves of books lined the walls, stretching from floor to ceiling. Ancient scrolls lay unrolled on heavy wooden tables, their intricate script a testament to centuries of accumulated knowledge. Globes depicted maps of worlds, some familiar, some unknown. This was a mind's sanctuary, a place of study and contemplation. This was Lorcan's lair.

Lyra moved quickly, efficiently. She wasn't looking for a treasure map or a grand confession. She was looking for patterns, for anomalies, for anything that hinted at the "vampire politics" Lorcan had alluded to, or the purpose behind the "selection ritual" beyond simple sustenance.

Her eyes scanned the cluttered desks. She found stacks of ledgers, their covers bound in dark leather. These were the first place to start. She opened one, her fingers skimming over the precise, elegant script. It contained meticulous records of past "selections" – names, origins, dates. And chillingly, their fates.

She flipped through pages, her heart a cold knot in her chest. Many names were marked with a simple "culled," confirming Melina's fate. Others were designated "assimilated," implying a transformation into a lesser, enslaved vampire. But what caught her eye were the discrepancies. Several names were marked with question marks, or simply left blank, with no indication of their final destination. And some, very few, had cryptic notations next to them: *"Observed. Retained. For other purpose."*

Her gaze snapped to the dates. The "retained" entries often corresponded to years when the selection ritual seemed to undergo subtle changes, shifts in the number of offerings or the specific "tests." This was more than just a feeding ritual; it was a complex, evolving system. And it had been manipulated.

Lyra flipped further back, to the oldest ledgers. Her fingers froze on a page dated nearly two decades ago. Her parents' names weren't here, of course. They weren't offerings. But there was an entry about a "deviant selection," a "breach of protocol." A family, marked for extermination due to "unforeseen complications." The names weren't listed, but the context was chillingly specific. A house, a forest, a "failure to comply."

She felt a surge of cold fury. This was it. This was the truth she sought, hidden in plain sight within Lorcan's meticulously kept records. Her family hadn't been killed arbitrarily. They had been caught in a "protocol breach," a consequence of the very system that now held her captive. And the orchestrator of this system, the "Minotaur" at the center of Lorcan's maze, was still hidden.

Her eyes darted around the room, searching for more clues. Her gaze landed on a smaller, intricately carved wooden box on a corner table – the same box Lorcan had been holding during their conversation. *Be wary of gifts, especially those that glitter.* He had been holding a clue, right there, in front of her.

Lyra approached the box. It wasn't locked. She opened it carefully. Inside, nestled on a bed of faded velvet, was a single, ancient, dried flower, pressed flat. And beneath it, a sheaf of faded parchment, brittle with age.

She unfolded the parchment carefully. It was a map, hand-drawn, of Sinful Castle. But it wasn't just a map of the known areas. It showed hidden passages, secret rooms, and what looked like a sprawling, subterranean network of tunnels and chambers. And several locations were circled, marked with symbols she recognized from the older, unsettling tapestries in the quieter corridors. These were places of ancient power, of ritual. And one of them, deep below the castle, was marked with the same half-closed eye symbol as the door to this very study.

But it was the small, handwritten notes scrawled in the margins that chilled her to the bone. They were Lorcan's elegant script, brief and cryptic. *"Arkyn's influence grows." "The Master's manipulation of the blood-rite." "The true purpose of the selections."* And, most ominously, *"He seeks the final key. The blood of the Unbroken."*

The blood of the Unbroken. Lyra's bloodline. Her family was known for its resilience, its uncanny ability to resist certain types of magic, certain forms of control. It was a secret, a legacy passed down through generations. And Arkyn, the ancient, shadowy leader, was somehow aware of it. He was seeking something from them, something that could only be extracted through this monstrous ritual.

A soft click echoed from the door. Lyra froze. Someone was coming. She quickly folded the map, stuffing it into the hidden pocket of her dress, along with the lock-picks. She closed the wooden box, replacing the dried flower. She moved back towards the entrance, her heart pounding a frantic rhythm. She was exposed.

The door creaked open, and Lorcan stepped inside. He paused, his twilight eyes sweeping over the room, then settling on Lyra. He didn't seem surprised to see her there. In fact, there was a subtle, almost knowing glint in his gaze.

"Trouble sleeping, Lyra Virellan?" he asked, his voice calm, devoid of accusation.

Lyra met his gaze. "Just... admiring your library, Lord Lorcan," she said, her voice steady despite the adrenaline coursing through her veins. "It's quite extensive."

He walked further into the room, his eyes lingering on the very spot where she had been looking at the ledgers. He didn't seem to notice the subtly disturbed stack of papers, or perhaps he chose not to.

"Indeed," he murmured, his gaze falling on the wooden box on the table. He picked it up, running his thumb over its surface, then glanced at her, a knowing look in his eyes. "Knowledge, Lyra, is a heavy burden. Especially the knowledge of secrets."

Lyra held his gaze. "Some secrets," she countered, "are meant to be uncovered."

A faint, melancholic smile touched his lips. "Perhaps. But uncovering them can be dangerous. Especially when those secrets are written in bone." He paused, then his eyes flickered towards her, a subtle hint of urgency in their depths. "You should return to your chambers, Lyra. It will be dawn soon. And shadows, no matter how deep, eventually retreat."

It was a clear dismissal, but also a warning. Lyra understood. She had found what she came for, or at least a significant piece of it. Lorcan had allowed her to find it. He was an informant, perhaps even an ally, in his own quiet, cryptic way. He was allowing her to play her game, giving her the pieces she needed to fight back against Arkyn's manipulations.

"Thank you for the... tour, Lord Lorcan," Lyra said, her voice sincere.

He simply nodded, his gaze distant, his expression unreadable.

Lyra slipped past him and out the door, closing it silently behind her. As she navigated the silent corridors back to Cassian's chambers, the cold fury in her heart burned hotter than ever. Arkyn. The true enemy. The one who had orchestrated her family's demise, and who now sought to control her blood.

The map in her pocket felt heavy, a burden of knowledge and a powerful tool. The secrets written in bone, the ancient machinations of Arkyn, were slowly coming to light. The price of blood was not just a debt; it was a legacy of pain and a path to vengeance. Lyra knew what she had to do. The game had shifted from survival to war.

Chapter 11: A Bed Made of Chains

The faint light of dawn painted the castle windows in hues of bruised purple and gray as Lyra returned to Cassian's chambers. Her heart still pounded with the adrenaline of her clandestine mission, and the parchment map of Sinful Castle, now tucked safely into her hidden pocket, felt like a burning secret against her skin. The knowledge she'd gained from Lorcan's study was a game-changer. Arkyn. The Blood of the Unbroken. The true purpose of the selections. It all pointed to a larger, more sinister plot than simple vengeance.

She slipped back into the opulence of Cassian's room, her senses alert. He wasn't there. The vast crimson bed was undisturbed, the fire in the hearth glowing low. A wave of exhaustion, both physical and mental, washed over her. She resisted the urge to collapse onto the bed. She wouldn't truly be safe until she was outside these walls, or until her mission was complete.

Lyra took a quick, cold wash at the basin, trying to clear her head. The bite mark on her neck still throbbed, a constant, tangible reminder of Cassian's claim. It was an unsettling duality: the mark of her captivity, yet also a strange, exhilarating sensation she was still trying to reconcile.

Just as she finished, the main doors to Cassian's chamber swung open. Cassian himself entered, a lean, dark silhouette against the brightening corridor. He looked immaculate, as always, but his golden eyes held a weary, almost shadowed intensity that spoke of a long night. He paused, his gaze sweeping over the room, then landing on Lyra. He hadn't expected her to be awake, she realized.

"Up early, little mortal?" he murmured, his voice a low, gravelly sound, deeper than usual. "Or did you have trouble sleeping after our... dance?"

Lyra met his gaze, refusing to show any signs of her secret excursion. "A light sleeper," she countered, her voice calm. "And the castle tends to creak."

He chuckled, a dry, humorless sound. "Indeed. Old stones tell many tales." His eyes, however, seemed to probe deeper, searching her expression. Lyra held firm, her features betraying nothing.

He walked past her, towards a heavy oak door Lyra hadn't noticed before, subtly blended into the wall near the fireplace. It was simpler, less ornate than the others, almost utilitarian. He opened it, revealing a dimly lit passage leading to... somewhere. The air emanating from it was colder, damper.

"Come," he commanded, his voice holding an unusual edge. "You spoke of breaking rules. Of challenging limits. Tonight, we shall see how far you are willing to go."

Lyra's heart gave a sudden lurch. This wasn't a choice; it was an order. And the tone of his voice, combined with the ominous entrance, sent a shiver of apprehension down her spine. This wasn't another dance or an interrogation. This felt different. More direct. More… primal.

She followed him, her hand instinctively brushing against the concealed dagger. The passage was narrow, winding downwards, deeper into the castle's foundations. The air grew heavy, smelling of damp earth and stale magic. The flickering light from Cassian's hand, which now held a small, glowing orb, cast dancing shadows on the rough-hewn stone walls.

They descended several levels, the silence broken only by the rhythmic echo of their footsteps. Finally, the passage opened into a larger, circular chamber.

This room was nothing like the opulence above. It was stark, made entirely of rough, unpolished stone. The only light came from a few strategically placed braziers, their flames casting a flickering, hellish glow. In the center of the chamber, raised slightly on a stone platform, was a large, heavy bed.

But it wasn't a bed for comfort. It was a bed made of chains.

Thick, polished iron chains were bolted to the stone at strategic points, radiating outwards from the center. Some were attached to heavy wrist and ankle cuffs, others simply dangled, waiting. The cold, raw iron glinted menacingly in the dim light. There were no sheets, no pillows, just the bare, chilling stone platform and the unforgiving metal. It was a place of punishment. A place of absolute control.

Lyra felt a cold dread spread through her. Her breath hitched. This was the "punishment room" she had heard whispers about. A place where the defiant were broken. Where limits were truly tested.

Cassian walked to the edge of the chained bed, his back to her. His silhouette was formidable against the fiery glow of the braziers. He didn't turn. He simply waited.

"A bed made of chains," he finally said, his voice a low, almost satisfied purr that echoed eerily in the silent chamber. "Designed for those who crave control. For those who believe they can defy it." He paused, then turned, his golden eyes blazing with an intense, possessive light. "You said you wished to be unbound, Lyra Virellan. Tonight, we shall see if that desire holds true when faced with… unbreakable bonds."

Lyra stared at the chains, then at him. He was challenging her. Not just physically, but psychologically. He wanted to see if her defiance, her resilience, was truly unbreakable.

"You plan to chain me?" Lyra asked, her voice calm despite the tremor of apprehension that ran through her. She kept her posture straight, her chin raised.

"Not if you choose not to be," he replied, a subtle, dangerous smirk on his lips. "It is a room of… exploration. Of limits.

Your limits." He gestured to the chains. "Every chain has a purpose, little mortal. To bind. To hold. To… compel."

He took a step towards her, his movements slow, deliberate, like a predator circling its prey. Lyra stood her ground, refusing to retreat.

"You wished to know my rules," he continued, his voice dropping to a seductive whisper, his golden eyes fixed on hers. "One of them is simple: obedience. But I prefer… willing obedience. An exploration of boundaries, not a forced submission."

He stopped mere inches from her, his tall frame looming over her. The heat from the braziers mingled with the chill of the chains, creating a strange, disorienting atmosphere. Lyra could feel his presence, powerful and overwhelming, pulling at her, trying to dominate her will.

"You expect me to… lie on that?" Lyra said, a hint of dry sarcasm in her voice, a desperate attempt to regain control of the narrative. "Chains? I'm flattered. You planned ahead."

A low chuckle escaped Cassian, a genuine, surprised sound. The tension, for a fleeting moment, dissipated, replaced by a flicker of his dangerous amusement. "Always planning, Lyra Virellan. Especially for my… most interesting acquisitions." He reached out, his hand hovering inches from her face, his long fingers flexing. "Do you truly believe you are so… unbound?"

Lyra held his gaze, her heart pounding. This was a test of wills, a dangerous dance of psychological warfare. She knew he wanted a reaction, a break in her composure.

"I believe," Lyra said, her voice dropping to a low, challenging whisper, "that true freedom is not about breaking chains, but about recognizing that they are merely… decorative." She held his gaze, a subtle defiance in her eyes. "You can bind my body, Lord Cassian. But you cannot bind my will. And that… is a freedom you can never truly possess."

Cassian stared at her, his golden eyes blazing with a potent mix of frustration, desire, and a grudging admiration. He didn't immediately respond. He seemed to be weighing her words, searching for a flaw in her logic, a crack in her resolve.

Then, a slow, predatory smile spread across his lips, revealing the tips of his fangs. "A fascinating philosophy, little mortal," he purred, his voice laced with dark amusement. "But as your body learns to crave what binds it, so too shall your will. The chains are merely an invitation to explore… deeper desires."

He stepped back, gesturing towards the chained bed. "Consider it… an offer. A chance to explore the boundaries of your own defiance. Or, perhaps, to discover a new kind of pleasure in surrender." His eyes held a challenging glint. "The choice, for now, is yours."

Lyra looked at the chains, then back at Cassian. He wasn't forcing her, not yet. He was tempting her, challenging her to enter his world of exquisite control. This was his game. And Lyra, with the map of secrets heavy in her pocket and the burning desire for vengeance in her heart, knew she had to play. She had to understand every facet of his power, every layer of his twisted desires, to ultimately turn them against him.

With a deep breath, Lyra walked towards the chained bed. She wouldn't surrender. But she would explore. She would learn. She would gather information. And in doing so, she would prove that even in a bed made of chains, her will, her spirit, remained utterly unbroken.

Chapter 12: Feeding the Flame

Lyra approached the bed made of chains, her steps slow and deliberate. The raw iron glinted ominously in the brazier light, promising restraint and discomfort. She didn't lie down immediately. Instead, she traced the cold metal with her fingertips, feeling the weight and strength of each link. Cassian watched her, his golden eyes unwavering, a silent challenge in their depths.

"So," she said, her voice calm, a subtle defiance in her tone. "Are these for me, or are you hoping to redecorate?"

Cassian chuckled, a low, satisfied sound. "For you, little mortal. Exclusively. And as for redecorating, I find their current arrangement… quite stimulating." He gestured towards the various cuffs. "Choose your preference. Or allow me to make the choice for you."

Lyra met his gaze. He wanted her to participate in her own subjugation, to acknowledge his control. She wouldn't give him that satisfaction entirely. But she would play his game, on her own terms.

She chose the wrist cuffs first, placing her hands, palms down, on the cool stone platform. The heavy iron clicked as she secured them, a surprisingly snug fit. Then, her ankles. The chains were long enough to allow some movement, but certainly not escape. She lay back, feeling the cold, unforgiving stone beneath her, the weight of the chains a tangible presence. Her body was confined, but her mind remained free, alert.

"Comfortable?" Cassian purred, walking closer, his shadow falling over her.

"As a queen on her throne," Lyra retorted, a wry smile touching her lips. "Just… a very minimalist throne."

He let out a soft, amused laugh, shaking his head. "You truly are a contradiction, Lyra Virellan." He knelt beside the bed, his face mere inches from hers, his golden eyes dark with a potent mix of desire and predatory amusement. His fingers brushed a strand of hair from her face, a shockingly tender gesture from such a brutal being.

"Tell me," he whispered, his voice a low, intimate rumble, "what do you feel, confined like this? Fear? Helplessness?"

Lyra held his gaze, refusing to be intimidated. "Curiosity," she replied, her voice steady. "And a desire to understand what makes you… tick. Or, perhaps, what makes you crave this much control."

His eyes widened almost imperceptibly, a flicker of surprise. He hadn't expected such directness. "A dangerous line of inquiry, little mortal."

"Knowledge is power, Lord Cassian," she countered softly, her gaze unwavering. "And I believe in acquiring as much as possible."

He watched her for a long moment, then a slow, predatory smile spread across his lips, revealing the tips of his fangs. "Indeed. And tonight, I shall teach you a different kind of knowledge. The knowledge of… exquisite surrender."

He leaned in, his lips brushing against her neck, just below the mark of their first bite. Lyra felt a shiver, a strange anticipation. This was it. The moment of truth.

Suddenly, a piercing, desperate scream echoed from somewhere above, from the higher levels of the castle. It was a woman's scream, full of terror and agony, followed by a guttural roar that vibrated through the very stone of the chamber.

Cassian froze. His head snapped up, his golden eyes blazing with an abrupt, almost feral intensity. The shift was immediate, instantaneous. The amused, seductive predator was gone, replaced by a creature of raw, untamed power. His fangs elongated visibly, gleaming in the brazier light.

"What was that?" Lyra whispered, a prickle of alarm running down her spine. The sound had been utterly chilling.

"An… unscheduled interruption," Cassian snarled, his voice guttural, laced with a potent fury. He stood abruptly, his gaze fixed on the entrance to the passage. "Stay here." It was a command, laced with an implicit threat.

He strode towards the entrance, his powerful form radiating an aura of barely contained rage. Lyra watched him go, feeling a mix of confusion and a strange sense of relief. The tension of their intimate confrontation had been broken, but replaced by a new, more immediate danger.

Moments later, another scream ripped through the silence, closer this time, followed by the sounds of a struggle, a crash, and a low, menacing growl. Then, silence. An oppressive, terrifying silence.

Lyra's mind raced. What was happening? An attack? A rogue vampire? This was not part of the ritual. This was chaos.

Suddenly, a figure appeared in the passage entrance, looming in the shadows. It wasn't Cassian. It was another vampire, larger than Cassian, with broad shoulders and a brutish, snarling face. His eyes were red, glazed with bloodlust, and his clothing was torn, stained with fresh crimson. He was clearly in a frenzy, his fangs fully extended, dripping saliva. A rogue.

He lumbered into the chamber, his gaze immediately falling on Lyra, chained to the bed. His eyes widened, a guttural growl escaping him. He smelled her blood, her vulnerability. He saw an easy meal.

"Mine," he snarled, his voice thick with unhinged hunger. He lunged towards her, his movements clumsy, yet powered by raw, bestial strength.

Lyra's heart hammered. This was unexpected. This was not Cassian's controlled game. This was a feral beast, driven by unchecked Thirst. She was chained, vulnerable. But she was not helpless.

As the rogue vampire approached, Lyra forced herself to remain calm. She assessed the distance, the chains, the vampire's uncontrolled movements. He was strong, yes, but sloppy. And she was clever.

"Don't come any closer," Lyra warned, her voice firm, cutting through his growls. "You don't want to do this."

He ignored her, a feral grin splitting his face, revealing rows of razor-sharp teeth. "Sweet blood!" he roared, lunging again, his hand reaching for her neck.

Just as his clawed fingers were about to close around her throat, Lyra moved. With a sudden, explosive burst of strength, she twisted her body, using the limited slack in the chains. She kicked out, her bare foot slamming into the vampire's knee with surprising force. He stumbled, letting out a roar of pain and surprise.

He lunged again, enraged. This time, Lyra anticipated his move. As he came within reach, she used the chains. With a swift, practiced motion, she twisted her wrist, pulling on the chain attached to her left hand. The chain, stretched taut, caught the vampire's outstretched arm, momentarily binding him.

He roared, thrashing wildly, trying to tear free. Lyra held firm, her muscles screaming with effort. This was her chance.

"You want my blood?" Lyra challenged, her voice ringing with defiance. "Come and get it, then. But you'll have to earn it."

She used her free right hand, which had slightly more mobility. Her eyes scanned the room, searching for anything, any weapon. Her gaze landed on one of the braziers, its metal frame hot and heavy.

The rogue vampire roared again, pulling hard on the chain, threatening to dislocate Lyra's shoulder. He was too strong to hold indefinitely.

Think, Lyra, think!

Then, an idea, reckless but potentially effective. "Don't hate me because I'm smarter," she taunted, forcing a smirk onto her face. "Hate me because I look better bleeding."

The vampire, enraged by her defiance, lunged again, pulling the chain even tighter. Lyra braced herself. As he came into range, she used the momentum of his lunge, twisting her body and the chain, pulling him off balance. He stumbled forward, directly towards the hot brazier.

With a final, desperate surge of strength, Lyra yanked the chain. The vampire, still off balance and focused on reaching her, crashed headfirst into the brazier. The metal clanged, sending sparks flying, and a howl of pure agony ripped from the vampire's throat as his face slammed against the glowing hot coals. The scent of burning flesh filled the chamber, sickeningly sweet.

He thrashed, screaming, disoriented by the pain. It wasn't a kill, but it was enough. Enough to buy her time.

Just as the rogue vampire began to recover, Cassian appeared in the entrance, his golden eyes blazing, his fangs fully extended, dripping. He took in the scene – Lyra chained, the rogue vampire writhing in agony on the brazier – in a single, terrifying glance.

A guttural, furious roar ripped from Cassian's chest, a sound of pure, unadulterated rage that made the very stones tremble. This was not the amused, controlled predator. This was the monster beneath the mask, unleashed.

He moved with blinding speed, a dark blur. In a split second, he was on the rogue vampire, a whirlwind of fists and fury. He didn't bite him. He ripped into him, tearing, pummeling, a brutal, visceral display of overwhelming power. The rogue vampire didn't stand a chance. He was nothing but a broken puppet in Cassian's hands, swiftly, brutally silenced.

Cassian stood over the crumpled form of the rogue, his chest heaving, his golden eyes still blazing with primal fury. His hands were stained with blood, and his dark silk shirt was ripped. He was magnificent and terrifying, a creature of pure, destructive power.

He turned to Lyra, his eyes slowly losing some of their wildness, focusing on her. He stared at her, chained to the bed, her face flushed from exertion, a small, defiant smile still lingering on her lips. A fresh cut, a scratch from the rogue's claw, now bled a thin line on her cheek.

"You handled yourself... admirably," he finally growled, his voice still rough with adrenaline. He walked towards her, his gaze unwavering. He reached down, his strong fingers easily unclipping the chains from her wrists and ankles. The cold metal fell away, leaving her body feeling strangely light, yet still connected to the powerful vampire before her.

He reached out, his thumb gently wiping the thin line of blood from her cheek. His golden eyes, now returned to their usual calculating intensity, scanned her face, as if searching for something.

"You are unharmed?" he asked, his voice unexpectedly gruff with concern.

"Just a scratch," Lyra replied, her voice a little breathless. She looked at the crumpled form of the rogue vampire, then back at Cassian, at the blood on his hands, the feral glint still in his eyes. This was the monster, unleashed. And she had just witnessed its raw, terrifying power. She had seen the thirst, not for her blood, but for blood in general, for dominance, for the elimination of threats. And, perhaps, a hint of something protective.

She had played a dangerous game, fighting a powerful opponent while confined. And she had won. Cassian's eyes held a mixture of awe and something else, something akin to respect. She had fed his fascination, and perhaps, ignited a different kind of flame within him.

Chapter 13: The Price of Defiance

The primal fury in Cassian's golden eyes slowly receded, replaced by a calculating intensity as he looked at Lyra. The rogue vampire, now a lifeless heap on the cold stone floor, was a grim testament to Cassian's unleashed power. Lyra felt a strange mix of awe and terror. He was not just a predator; he was a force of nature.

He extended a hand, his touch surprisingly gentle, as he helped her sit up on the edge of the chained bed. The residual warmth from his palm sent a jolt through her, a startling contrast to the cold stone beneath her.

"Are you truly unharmed?" he asked again, his voice still rough, a lingering edge of the unleashed beast in its tone. He tilted her face up, his thumb gently tracing the faint scratch on her cheek.

"I've had worse," Lyra replied, her voice a little breathless, but steady. She met his gaze, a silent challenge in her eyes. "Your chains aren't as secure as you think, Lord Cassian."

A faint, almost imperceptible smirk touched his lips. "Perhaps. Or perhaps, little mortal, you possess an unexpected talent for… creative defiance." His eyes lingered on her face, then dropped to her throat, to the bite mark that pulsed faintly. "And a surprising resilience to pain."

He stood, pulling her up with him. Lyra felt a momentary dizziness, the lingering effects of the first bite combined with the adrenaline crash from her impromptu fight. She swayed slightly, and Cassian's arm instinctively went around her waist, steadying her. His body was hard, unyielding, a source of dangerous warmth.

"Come," he commanded, his voice softer now. "This place is no longer… suitable. And you require tending."

He led her out of the chamber, leaving the crumpled body of the rogue vampire behind. As they ascended the winding passage, Lyra's mind raced. The encounter had been terrifying, but also revelatory. She had seen Cassian's monstrousness, his capacity for unbridled violence. But she had also glimpsed something else: a flicker of concern, perhaps even a possessive protectiveness. It was a dangerous thought, but one she couldn't ignore.

They returned to Cassian's opulent chambers. The contrast between the cold, brutal dungeon and the luxurious bedchamber was jarring. Cassian led her to a plush chaise lounge near the fireplace and gently pushed her down onto it. He then moved to a small, ornate cabinet, retrieving a delicate glass vial filled with a shimmering, iridescent liquid and a soft, linen cloth.

He returned to her side, his gaze intense. "This will aid in your recovery," he murmured, uncorking the vial. The liquid smelled faintly of herbs and something metallic. He dipped the cloth into it, then carefully, gently, began to clean the small scratch on her cheek.

His touch was surprisingly tender, his long fingers surprisingly delicate. Lyra watched him, captivated by the unexpected softness of his actions. This was a side of Cassian she hadn't seen – the healer, the caretaker. It was a stark contrast to the brutal predator she had witnessed just moments before.

"Thank you," Lyra said, the words surprising even herself.

He merely grunted in response, his eyes fixed on the wound. Once he was satisfied, he leaned back, tossing the soiled cloth into the roaring fire. "You are reckless, Lyra Virellan," he stated, his voice now flat, devoid of emotion. "To provoke such a creature, while bound. It was… foolish."

Lyra met his gaze. "Foolish, perhaps. But effective. And I am not one to cower, Lord Cassian. Not even when facing death."

His golden eyes narrowed. "That defiance," he said, his voice low, almost a growl. "It could be your undoing. Or… your salvation." He paused, then stood, beginning to pace the room, his movements restless. "The other Lords… they will have heard. They will be watching."

"Let them," Lyra countered, pushing herself up from the chaise. The dizzying spell had passed, replaced by a renewed sense of purpose. "I came here for a reason. And I won't be broken by their expectations."

Cassian stopped pacing, turning to face her, his expression unreadable. "Such defiance carries a price, Lyra," he said, his voice grave. "A public price."

Just then, a soft knock echoed on the chamber doors. Cassian's eyes sharpened. "Enter," he commanded.

A cloaked vampire, one of the castle's seneschals, entered, bowing deeply. "My Lord. The High Lords request your presence, and that of the… offering. In the main hall. They wish to… address the matter of the recent disturbance. And to ensure… protocol is maintained."

Cassian's lips thinned. He understood. This wasn't a request; it was a summons. A public inquiry into the rogue vampire's attack, and a chance for the other Lords to reassert their authority, to humble Cassian, and to remind Lyra of her place.

He looked at Lyra, his golden eyes holding a silent question. "Ready for another audience, little mortal?"

Lyra's lips curved into a faint, defiant smile. "Always, Lord Cassian. I do enjoy a good show."

He let out a low, almost reluctant chuckle. "You are truly incorrigible." He offered her his arm, a gesture of public solidarity, a subtle declaration of his continued claim over her. Lyra took it, her fingers brushing against the cool, dark fabric of his sleeve.

As they walked towards the main hall, Lyra's mind raced. This was an opportunity. A chance to show the other vampires she was not to be easily intimidated. A chance to gather more information. And a chance to cement Cassian's position as her unlikely, possessive protector.

The main hall, where the first selection had taken place, was once again filled with vampires. But this time, the atmosphere was colder, more formal, less festive. The High Lords sat on a raised dais, their faces grim, their eyes fixed on Cassian and Lyra as they entered. Lorcan was among them, his expression as unreadable as ever, though his gaze held a flicker of something she couldn't quite decipher when it landed on her.

The High Lord who had presided over the earlier selection, the one with the granite face, cleared his throat. "Lord Cassian," he intoned, his voice resonating with authority. "There has been a breach in our sacred protocols. A rogue, unhinged creature, attacked an offering under your protection. This cannot go unpunished. And the offering herself… exhibited a dangerous degree of defiance."

Lyra felt the weight of their judgment, their cold, ancient eyes boring into her. They expected her to cower, to confess her fear, to be publicly broken.

"The rogue," Cassian interrupted, his voice cutting through the High Lord's with an effortless authority, "was dealt with. Swiftly. Decisively. My chambers, and my guests, are secure." His gaze was unwavering, challenging.

"And the offering's conduct?" another High Lord, ancient and wizened, interjected, his voice raspy. "She resisted. She provoked. She dared to… fight back." His eyes, like chips of ice, fixed on Lyra. "Such behavior is unheard of. A dangerous precedent."

Lyra felt a surge of defiance. This was their game. Their rules. But she had a voice.

"I merely defended myself, Lords," Lyra stated, her voice clear and strong, cutting through the hushed silence of the hall. "When faced with an unprovoked attack, is it not instinct to survive?"

A ripple went through the assembled vampires. Her directness, her lack of fear, was clearly shocking to them. Cassian, standing beside her, remained silent, his golden eyes watching her, a subtle hint of satisfaction in their depths.

"Instinct, perhaps," the High Lord with the granite face replied, his voice laced with disdain. "But mortals are expected to yield. To accept their fate. Not to… challenge the natural order."

"The natural order," Lyra retorted, her chin lifting defiantly, "is often merely an excuse for tyranny. I was attacked. I fought back. I survived. Is that not a strength you value, even in a mortal?" She looked directly at the High Lords, her gaze unwavering. "Or do you prefer your offerings to be… weak?"

A tense silence descended upon the hall. Her words, so openly defiant, so utterly without fear, reverberated through the ancient stones. The other offerings stared at her in wide-eyed disbelief. Some of the younger vampires seemed intrigued, a spark of admiration in their eyes. Even the High Lords seemed momentarily stunned by her audacity.

Cassian, standing beside her, let out a low, almost imperceptible hum of amusement. He squeezed her arm lightly, a silent signal of approval, of pride. He had brought her here to be publicly tested, publicly punished perhaps, but Lyra had turned it into a defiant declaration. She had not cowered. She had not broken. She had amazed them.

The High Lord with the granite face stared at Lyra, his eyes narrowing in cold assessment. He wanted to punish her, to crush her spirit. But he also saw the effect she was having, the quiet murmurs of surprise and respect among some of the younger vampires. And he saw Cassian's quiet, possessive satisfaction.

"Her spirit is… untamed," the High Lord finally declared, his voice still severe, but with a grudging concession. "A dangerous trait. But… she is Lord Cassian's. He will manage her. The protocol, Lord Cassian, dictates that her defiance must be… publicly acknowledged. A lesson for the others."

Cassian's lips curved into a slow, predatory smile. He looked at Lyra, his golden eyes blazing with a potent mix of possessive amusement and dark promise. "Indeed, High Lord," he purred, his voice resonating with power. "And I assure you, Lyra Virellan will learn her lessons. Most… intimately."

He turned to Lyra, his gaze intense. "Come, Lyra," he commanded, his voice a low, intimate whisper, meant only for her ears. "The price of defiance, little mortal, is often a very… personal one."

Lyra met his gaze, a defiant sparkle in her eyes. She had faced them all, unafraid. She had survived. And she had, against all odds, turned a public humiliation into a display of her unyielding spirit. The other offerings looked at her, not with pity, but with a nascent glimmer of hope. Lyra Virellan, the defiant mortal, had just shown them that even in the heart of darkness, one could still refuse to be broken.

Chapter 14: When Silence Screams

The public display of defiance had left Lyra strangely energized. She'd spent the remainder of the night in Cassian's chambers, though not in his company. He had left shortly after their return, presumably to deal with the lingering political fallout of the rogue vampire incident and her unprecedented insolence. Lyra used the time to rest, to let the lingering hum of his bite settle, and to review the secrets she'd gleaned from Lorcan's study. The map of hidden passages felt like a promise, a whisper of freedom within the castle's ancient bones.

The following day dawned with a subtle shift in the castle's atmosphere. The air felt heavier, quieter. The other offerings seemed to look at Lyra with a mixture of fear and a desperate, fragile hope. Her act of defiance had, unexpectedly, given them a glimpse of possibility.

Lyra spent the day in a state of heightened awareness, playing the part of the captive while internally strategizing. She explored Cassian's vast chambers, subtly testing doors, feeling for loose stones, cataloging every detail. The luxurious prison was designed to lull its occupants into a false sense of security, to make them forget the bars on the windows. Lyra refused to forget.

As dusk began to settle, painting the sky outside in hues of bruised purple, a soft knock echoed on the chamber doors. It wasn't the silent servant, nor Cassian's confident stride. Lyra's senses sharpened.

She opened the door to find Lorcan standing there. He was alone, his usual dark clothing blending almost seamlessly with the dimming light of the corridor. His twilight eyes, however, were wide awake, holding their familiar depth and quiet intensity. There was no guard, no pretense of a formal visit. This was something different.

"Lord Lorcan," Lyra greeted, keeping her voice neutral. She glanced instinctively down the corridor. It was empty.

He inclined his head slightly. "Lyra Virellan. May I enter?" His voice was a low, smooth baritone, calm and measured as always, but Lyra sensed a subtle urgency beneath it.

Lyra stepped aside, allowing him entry. She closed the door behind him, plunging the room into a more intimate quiet. The only sound was the crackle of the dying fire in the hearth.

Lorcan moved further into the room, his gaze sweeping over the opulent furnishings, then settling on Lyra. He didn't sit. He simply stood, a contemplative presence in the vast space.

"You caused quite a stir last night," he observed, his voice soft, almost a murmur. "Public defiance is… rare here. Especially from an offering."

"I merely expressed myself," Lyra countered, her lips curving into a faint, wry smile. "Some find it unsettling."

"Most find it suicidal," Lorcan corrected gently, his eyes holding hers. "Cassian, however, found it… amusing. And intriguing. That is dangerous for you, Lyra. His interest is a double-edged sword."

"I am aware," Lyra said, her voice cool. She crossed her arms, her stance defensive. "You warned me of shadows. And of gifts."

Lorcan nodded, his gaze distant, as if remembering something ancient. "Indeed. The deeper the shadow, the more subtle the blade. The sweeter the gift, the higher the price." He paused, then his eyes met hers again, a piercing intensity in their depths. "Do you truly understand what you have stepped into, Lyra? This is not merely a court of hungry beasts. This is a game of ancient, complex power. And you are a pawn, albeit a very… unpredictable one."

"I am no one's pawn," Lyra stated, her voice firm, unwavering. "I am here for a purpose. My purpose."

A faint, melancholic smile touched Lorcan's lips. "Such certainty. I once possessed it too." His gaze drifted to the intricate tapestries depicting the Vampire Wars, particularly one showing a warrior, bound in chains, being led before a masked figure. "Long ago," he continued, his voice softer, almost a whisper, "I too was… an offering. Chosen. Bound."

Lyra's eyes widened. She stared at him, stunned. Lorcan? The intellectual, the observer, the high-ranking Lord? An offering? It was unthinkable. He was so calm, so in control.

"You?" she whispered, her voice laced with disbelief.

He nodded, his gaze returning to her, holding a deep, ancient sadness. "Yes. Chosen. By the one who orchestrated this ritual, this… twisted theatre. By Arkyn."

The name hung in the air, a cold, heavy presence. Arkyn. The true enemy. The one Lyra had discovered in Lorcan's ledgers.

"Arkyn," Lyra repeated, her voice grim. "He manipulates this entire ritual. This 'selection' is a facade."

Lorcan's eyes seemed to darken further. "It is a means to an end. He seeks… something specific. A rare essence. A unique lineage." His gaze flickered to Lyra's neck, to the faint mark of Cassian's bite. "The Blood of the Unbroken."

Lyra felt a cold dread. He knew. He knew about her lineage.

"My family..." she began, her voice barely a whisper.

"Were not merely 'culled' for defying protocol," Lorcan interrupted, his voice grave. "They were… an obstacle. A powerful obstacle. Arkyn seeks to control what he cannot break. And your blood, Lyra, is a key component in his ultimate design."

He paused, his eyes searching her face. "He seeks to merge the essence of the Unbroken with ancient vampire power, to create something truly formidable. A weapon. A vessel for his own ambition. The selected females are merely… experiments. Attempts to find the right vessel, the right blend."

Lyra felt a chill run down her spine. Her blood was not just a debt; it was a target. Her very existence, a pawn in a terrifying grand scheme.

"And Cassian?" Lyra asked, her voice tight. "Does he know of Arkyn's true intentions? Or is he merely a… complacent participant?"

Lorcan's gaze softened, a hint of something complex, perhaps pity, entering his eyes. "Cassian… is bound by his own loyalties. And his own… thirst. He believes he controls the game. But Arkyn pulls the strings. Cassian is a warrior, Lyra. Powerful, yes. But sometimes… too focused on the immediate battle to see the deeper war."

He took a step closer, his voice dropping to an urgent whisper. "My selection, long ago, was a test. A lesson in breaking spirit. I survived. But I learned to move in the shadows. To gather information. To watch. And to wait. For someone like you."

Lyra stared at him, a sudden, blinding realization dawning. Lorcan wasn't just an observer; he was a silent rebel. He had been waiting for a chance, for someone brave enough, foolish enough, to challenge the system from within. He was offering her an alliance, a covert partnership against Arkyn.

"Why me?" Lyra asked, her voice barely audible.

"Because you defied him," Lorcan replied, his eyes burning with a quiet intensity. "Because you did not break. Because your spirit, Lyra, screams even in silence. And that is a song I thought I would never hear again." He paused, then inclined his head towards the hidden map in Lyra's pocket. "Did you find what you sought in my study?"

Lyra felt a surge of adrenaline. He knew. He had allowed her in. He had left the clues for her to find.

"I found… pieces," she admitted, her gaze unwavering. "Enough to know the maze is larger than I imagined. And the Minotaur, far more ancient."

A rare, almost genuine smile touched Lorcan's lips, a flicker of hope in his ancient eyes. "Indeed. The labyrinth is deep. But now, you have a thread. A path. Be careful, Lyra. Arkyn watches everyone. He controls the flow of information. He shapes narratives."

He took a step back, melting slightly into the shadows of the room. "I cannot openly defy him. Not yet. But I can… guide. I can illuminate. Just as the moonlight reveals paths hidden by the sun."

"What do you want from me?" Lyra asked, her voice low.

"Justice," Lorcan replied, his voice barely a whisper, yet resonating with an ancient weariness. "For those who were broken. For those who were consumed. And for a world that deserves to be free of his grasp." He looked at her, a profound plea in his eyes. "Expose him, Lyra. Break his control. Undo this ritual. Before he finds the final key."

A soft, almost imperceptible sound from the corridor outside. Lorcan's eyes sharpened. "Someone approaches," he murmured. "Remember what you have seen. What you have learned. And trust nothing that glitters."

He turned, melting into the shadows, his form blurring, then vanishing completely, leaving Lyra alone in the vast chamber. The silence screamed with the weight of the secrets he had just revealed, the chilling truth of Arkyn's machinations, and the unexpected alliance she had just forged.

Lyra walked to the window, gazing out at the deepening twilight. The castle, once a symbol of her singular vengeance, now felt like a giant, pulsing organism, a network of hidden plots and ancient betrayals. She was no longer just here for her family. She was here to expose a monster, to dismantle a system, and to free others. The burden was immense, but so was the newfound clarity. The quiet observation of Lorcan had opened her eyes. And now, she could truly begin to fight.

Chapter 15: Beneath His Thirst

The revelations from Lorcan had left Lyra reeling, yet strangely emboldened. The castle, once a straightforward target for vengeance, was now a complex web of ancient conspiracies, and she, unknowingly, was at its very heart. Arkyn, the blood of the Unbroken, the manipulated ritual – the pieces of the puzzle were finally clicking into place, painting a far more terrifying picture.

The morning after Lorcan's visit, Lyra awoke to a profound sense of isolation. Cassian was still absent, likely engaged in the intricate political machinations of the vampire court. The opulent chambers felt like a gilded cage, the silence pressing in around her, screaming with the weight of hidden truths.

She spent the day reviewing the mental map of Lorcan's study, piecing together the cryptic notes. The hidden passages, the ceremonial chambers deep beneath the castle – these were her new targets. But she needed a plan, and she needed more information about Arkyn's precise intentions and vulnerabilities.

As dusk began to settle, casting long, purple shadows across the lavish room, Lyra felt a familiar prickling sensation on her neck. The bite mark, still faintly visible, throbbed with a low, insistent hum. It was a call, a silent summons she had come to recognize. Cassian was coming.

She didn't have to wait long. The heavy chamber doors swung open, and Cassian strode in. He looked weary, a subtle tension etched around his golden eyes, yet his presence was as formidable as ever. He wore a simpler, dark tunic, open at the throat, revealing the powerful column of his neck.

He walked directly towards her, his gaze intense, assessing. Lyra met his eyes, refusing to show any apprehension. She noticed a faint trace of blood on his chin, fresh and dark. He had fed recently, but perhaps not fully, or perhaps from a source that hadn't satisfied him. There was a restless energy about him, a predatory hum that filled the air.

"You seem… thoughtful, little mortal," he murmured, his voice a low, gravelly sound. He stopped inches from her, his gaze dropping to her neck, to the mark. His eyes darkened with a raw, primal hunger. "Has the memory of our last encounter left its mark?"

Lyra's hand instinctively went to her neck. "It is certainly... memorable," she replied, her voice calm. "Like a persistent itch."

He let out a low chuckle, a deep, rumbling sound that vibrated through her. "An itch I intend to scratch, Lyra Virellan." His golden eyes blazed with a fierce intensity, a raw, unrestrained desire that made her blood hum in response. "Tonight, the formalities are done. The games are over."

He reached out, his hand grasping her chin, tilting her head back, exposing her throat. His touch was cold, yet it sent a wave of heat through her. Lyra felt her heart pound, a frantic drum against her ribs. This was different. This was not the measured, controlled bite of the "test." This was something wilder, more primal.

"My thirst has grown," he stated, his voice a low growl, "and your defiance has only made it sharper. Tonight, I will not hold back."

Lyra stared into his golden eyes, seeing not just hunger, but a tempest of powerful emotions swirling within them. There was possessiveness, yes, and a fierce, almost desperate need. This was the monster, stripped of its mask, giving in to its primal urges.

She felt the brush of his lips, cold and firm, against her neck. Then, the piercing sensation as his fangs sank deep into her flesh. It was a sharp, searing pain, far more intense than the first time. Lyra gasped, her body tensing, every nerve ending screaming.

But then, as his lips molded to her skin, and she felt the powerful suction as he drew her blood, the pain began to recede, replaced by an overwhelming, intoxicating wave of pure, unadulterated pleasure. It was a dizzying rush, a fiery current that spread through her veins, dissolving all thought, all resistance. Her muscles went limp, her breath hitched, and a soft, involuntary moan escaped her lips.

It was unlike anything she had ever experienced. A terrifying surrender, yet utterly blissful. She felt herself floating, her senses overwhelmed, the world blurring around the edges. Her blood, her very essence, was being drawn from her, and her body, impossibly, craved more.

She felt him pull back, a wet, intimate sound as his fangs disengaged. The sudden absence of his lips, of the suction, left her feeling lightheaded, profoundly empty, yet strangely sated. Her legs buckled, and she would have fallen if Cassian hadn't caught her, his strong arms wrapping around her waist, holding her upright against his powerful body.

She leaned against him, her head resting against his shoulder, utterly spent. The world seemed to swim before her eyes, and her thoughts were a confused jumble of pleasure and shock.

The bite mark on her neck throbbed, a hot, aching pulse, but it was also a lingering echo of that intoxicating euphoria.

Cassian held her, his chest heaving faintly. He pulled her closer, his lips brushing against her hair, then against the wound on her neck, a possessive, almost reverent touch. He inhaled deeply, the scent of her blood, mingled with the lingering echo of his own power, filling his senses.

"Mine," he murmured, his voice husky, thick with the aftermath of his feeding. "Utterly mine."

Lyra, still disoriented, found her breath. She looked up at him, her eyes a little hazy, but with a spark of her usual defiance. She saw the raw satisfaction in his golden eyes, the lingering hunger, but also a profound, almost primal contentment. He had given in to his thirst, and she had experienced its full, overwhelming power.

A wave of unexpected, almost perverse humor washed over her. She had been completely at his mercy, utterly consumed, and yet... she had survived. And even found a strange, dark pleasure in it.

"Well," Lyra managed, her voice a little weak, but with a wry grin. She reached up, her fingers lightly touching the side of his mouth, where a faint smear of her blood still stained his perfect skin. "Next time, Lord Cassian, we should put a napkin on. You're a messy eater."

Cassian froze, his golden eyes widening in a mixture of disbelief and a rekindled, dangerous amusement. He stared at her, at her blood on his lips, at her weak yet utterly defiant grin. Then, a low, rumbling chuckle started in his chest, growing into a full, throaty laugh that filled the chamber, shaking his powerful frame.

"By the Ancestors," he gasped, still laughing, his eyes bright with a potent mix of astonishment and delight. "You truly are… incomparable, Lyra Virellan." He leaned down, his lips brushing against hers, a whisper of a kiss, tasting of her own blood and his power. "Even when bleeding, you find a way to defy me."

He tightened his arms around her, pulling her into an even closer embrace, a possessive, triumphant gesture. Lyra leaned into him, her body still weak, but her spirit unbroken. She had faced his unleashed hunger, had been consumed by it, and had emerged with her wit intact. The second bite, far from breaking her, had only intensified the strange, dangerous connection between them. It was a bond forged in blood and defiance, a paradox of pain and pleasure that had just become undeniably, terrifyingly real.

Chapter 16: My Name on His Tongue

The aftermath of Cassian's unrestrained feeding left Lyra both physically weakened and mentally reeling. The potent blend of pain and pleasure still hummed beneath her skin, a disorienting echo that confused her senses and challenged her every preconceived notion about her captor. She lay in his arms, utterly spent, listening to the powerful, steady beat of his heart against her ear.

He held her close, his breathing deep and even, a possessive weight that was both suffocating and, to her utter bewilderment, strangely comforting. His scent, a mix of old leather, metallic blood, and something uniquely his, filled her nostrils. It was the scent of danger, of power, of the very monster she had come to destroy. Yet, nestled against him, a part of her felt... safe. It was a terrifying realization, a betrayal of her own carefully constructed defenses.

Time seemed to stretch, moments blurring into an eternity of intimate silence. Lyra felt herself drifting, suspended between consciousness and a strange, blood-induced haze. She fought it, forcing her mind to focus, to reassert control. She was here for vengeance, not for comfort.

Then, his voice, a low rumble from deep in his chest, vibrated through her. "Lyra."

It was soft, unexpected. Not the commanding roar, not the teasing purr, but something gentle, almost hesitant. He hadn't just called her "little mortal" or "defiant one." He had spoken her name. Her *true* name. And the way he said it, infused with a tenderness she hadn't heard from him before, sent an inexplicable shiver down her spine. It was a name spoken not to command or to threaten, but to acknowledge. To truly see.

Lyra stirred, tilting her head slightly to look at him. His golden eyes, no longer blazing with hunger, were now soft, reflective, almost... vulnerable. He was gazing down at her, his expression a complex mix of something akin to concern, satisfaction, and a deep, ancient emotion she couldn't quite decipher.

"Are you... well?" he murmured, his thumb brushing lightly against the healing mark on her neck, sending a fresh wave of unexpected warmth through her.

Lyra blinked, surprised by his apparent solicitude. "I will recover," she said, her voice a little hoarse, but regaining its steady tone. "Your appetite is... formidable."

A faint, almost embarrassed smile touched his lips, a truly human expression. "It has been... long since I fed so completely. So... profoundly." His gaze intensified, fixed on hers. "Your blood, Lyra. It is... unique. Potent. It sings to me in a way no other has."

Lyra felt a strange blush creep up her neck. It was more than just physical hunger for him, she realized. Her blood resonated with something within him, something ancient and deeply buried. Lorcan's words about the "Blood of the Unbroken" echoed in her mind. This was not just about sustenance; it was about connection. A dangerous, intoxicating connection.

"Does it taste of defiance, then?" she challenged softly, trying to regain some of her usual composure.

He chuckled, a low, warm sound. "And something else. Something wild. Unbroken." He paused, his golden eyes searching hers, delving deeper than any words could. "You have surprised me, Lyra Virellan. You came here not as a lamb, but as a wolf. And yet… you did not break. Even under my full Thirst."

Lyra held his gaze. This was a moment of unexpected vulnerability from him, a rare glimpse beneath his layers of control and cruelty. She had to use it wisely.

"What did you expect?" Lyra asked, her voice quiet. "For me to shatter? To plead?"

"Most do," he admitted, his voice barely a whisper. "Most crumble. But you… you defied me even as I took your blood. You still had the wit to mock me." He shook his head slightly, a faint smile on his lips. "It is… disarming."

He shifted, pulling her closer still, his arm tightening around her waist. "You are not like the others, Lyra," he repeated, the words holding a weight of conviction she hadn't heard before. "You challenge me. You intrigue me. And that… is a very dangerous thing for both of us."

Lyra felt a shiver, not of fear, but of a strange, unsettling awareness. He was acknowledging the bond, the complex current that ran between them. He was seeing her, truly seeing her, for the first time not as an offering or a target, but as an individual who had captivated his ancient, jaded heart.

"What happens now?" Lyra asked, her voice softer than she intended, a hint of genuine uncertainty creeping in.

He was silent for a long moment, his gaze distant, thoughtful. "Now," he murmured, his voice laced with a subtle promise, "we begin. The real lessons. The true understanding. You sought to know my rules. And I... seek to understand your unbound spirit."

He lowered his head, his lips brushing against the pulse point on her neck, a soft, almost tender kiss that sent a fresh wave of warmth through her. It was not a bite, not a threat, but a claim. A mark of possession.

"You are mine, Lyra Virellan," he whispered, the words resonating with a possessive power that went beyond physical ownership. "Not as a prisoner, not as a plaything. But as... something more." He pulled back slightly, his golden eyes burning into hers, filled with an intensity that promised both ecstasy and inevitable pain. "My fascination. My challenge. My... undoing."

Lyra stared at him, breathless. His words, "My undoing," echoed in the silent chamber, a chilling prophecy. He saw her as something that could unravel him, something that could break through his centuries of control. And that, Lyra realized, was a potent weapon. Her name, spoken so gently, so intimately, had just become a key.

She was no longer just the girl seeking vengeance. She was Lyra, the one who intrigued Cassian, the one who challenged him, the one who had seen the monster beneath his mask and found a wounded soul beneath. The lines were blurring, the purpose shifting. Her heart, once solely consumed by hatred, felt a strange, unsettling flutter. The game had just become infinitely more personal.

Chapter 17: The Bite I Didn't Hate

The quiet intimacy of Cassian's confession, his use of her name, and the unsettling truth of "My undoing," left Lyra in a state of profound disarray. The carefully constructed walls around her heart, forged in the fires of vengeance, felt dangerously permeable. She had come here to kill, to destroy, yet in the heart of the beast's lair, she found herself grappling with an emotion she hadn't anticipated: a bewildering, terrifying, and undeniably potent attraction.

The days that followed were a blur of new routines within the gilded prison of Cassian's chambers. He was a constant, formidable presence. He no longer left her for long stretches, his golden eyes often finding her, observing her, an unspoken claim in their depths. The initial formality between them began to erode, replaced by a strange, compelling rhythm.

He would engage her in conversations, not about the selection ritual or the court, but about history, philosophy, the fleeting nature of mortal lives. Lyra found herself responding, drawn into debates that sharpened her wit and exposed new facets of Cassian's ancient, complex mind. He was far more than a bloodthirsty monster; he was a being of immense intellect, centuries of knowledge, and a loneliness that occasionally, fleetingly, seeped through his formidable control.

The intimate moments continued, too. Sometimes, he would simply sit and watch her, his gaze intense, possessive, yet devoid of immediate hunger. Other times, he would touch her, a brush of his fingers on her arm, a hand on the small of her back as they walked through the chambers. These touches were not overtly sexual, but they were charged with a potent awareness, a constant reminder of the physical connection forged in blood.

One evening, as twilight bled into night, casting the room in a soft, ethereal glow, Lyra found herself reading one of Cassian's ancient tomes – a collection of forgotten mortal poetry. She sat by the roaring fireplace, the heavy book open on her lap, its parchment brittle with age. Cassian was across from her, seemingly lost in his own thoughts, a glass of blood shimmering darkly in his hand.

Lyra's neck still throbbed faintly from the last bite, a phantom echo of pleasure and pain. She traced the mark with her fingers, a subtle, almost unconscious gesture.

"Does it still bother you?" Cassian's voice cut through the silence, soft and low.

Lyra looked up. His golden eyes were fixed on her, contemplative. "It is… a constant reminder," she replied, choosing her words carefully.

He rose from his chair and walked towards her, his movements silent, fluid. He knelt beside her chair, his gaze fixed on her neck. "And what does it remind you of?" he murmured, his voice husky.

Lyra met his gaze. The truth was unsettling. It reminded her not just of her captivity, but of the dizzying, forbidden pleasure, the strange connection she had felt. It reminded her that the lines were blurring, that her hatred was becoming intertwined with something else.

"It reminds me," she said, her voice dropping to a whisper, "that I am still here. Still… defiant." It was a half-truth, a desperate attempt to maintain her facade.

A faint, almost imperceptible smile touched his lips. "And I would have it no other way." He reached out, his long fingers gently cupping her chin, tilting her head. His golden eyes, now dark with hunger, locked onto hers. "Tonight, Lyra Virellan, I will take from you again. But this time… I wish for more than just sustenance."

Lyra felt her heart quicken, a familiar surge of adrenaline. This was not a test. This was not a punishment. This was an invitation, unspoken yet undeniable. And to her shock, a part of her felt a profound, almost desperate anticipation. The thought of his fangs, of that intoxicating rush, sent a shiver through her.

He leaned in, his lips brushing against her neck, just below her ear, sending goosebumps down her arms. His breath was cool against her skin, and she could feel the subtle shift as his fangs extended, razor-sharp points against her flesh.

"Allow me," he whispered, his voice a silken seduction, "to show you the true depth of the bond we forge in blood. To show you… the pleasure."

Lyra closed her eyes, a shiver running through her. She didn't resist. She didn't fight. For the first time, she simply… allowed it. A choice, born of a bewildering desire, not of fear.

His fangs pierced her skin, a sharp, momentary sting, followed instantly by that familiar, overwhelming wave of euphoric pleasure. It was stronger this time, more potent, dissolving her thoughts, her resistance, until only sensation remained. Her body arched, a soft gasp escaping her lips, and her fingers clenched, not in pain, but in a desperate grip on the fabric of her dress.

She felt him draw, a slow, rhythmic pull that emptied her, yet filled her with an indescribable bliss. Every nerve ending sang, and her vision exploded with a kaleidoscope of colors behind her closed eyelids. It was terrifyingly intimate, an invasion of her very being, yet she welcomed it, craving the intoxicating release.

He deepened the bite, drawing more, infusing her with a strange, dark current that hummed through her veins, a fusion of his power and her essence. She felt herself spiraling, falling into a delicious abyss of sensation, utterly lost in the moment.

Then, slowly, he pulled back. The suction ceased, the exquisite pressure lifted. Lyra gasped, her eyes fluttering open. She felt dizzy, weak, but utterly, profoundly sated. The mark on her neck throbbed, a hot, aching pulse, but it was accompanied by a deep, lingering warmth that spread through her entire body.

She looked up at Cassian. His golden eyes were dark, almost black, pupils dilated with the aftermath of his feeding. His lips were stained crimson, and his chest was heaving faintly. He looked utterly consumed, satiated, and terrifyingly beautiful. He was looking at her, his gaze filled with a raw, primal satisfaction, and something else – a deep, unsettling possessiveness that made her tremble.

Lyra reached up, her fingers brushing against the side of his mouth, just as she had before. But this time, it wasn't a challenge or a quip. It was a soft, almost reverent touch. The blood felt warm and strangely familiar against her skin.

She met his gaze, her heart pounding a strange, unfamiliar rhythm. The hatred that had fueled her for so long felt... distant. Blurred. Overwhelmed by this potent, forbidden connection.

A single thought echoed in her mind, clear and undeniable, shocking her to her core. *I didn't hate that bite.*

She saw a flicker of surprise in Cassian's eyes, as if he had read her very thoughts. He leaned in, his lips brushing against hers, tasting of her own blood, of his power, of something ancient and undeniable. It was not a gentle kiss, but a deep, hungry fusion, a silent promise of everything she now felt.

He pulled back, his golden eyes blazing with a triumphant, possessive light. "You feel it, Lyra Virellan," he murmured, his voice husky with satisfaction. "The bond. The truth beneath the thirst."

Lyra could only stare at him, breathless, her body still humming with the aftershocks of the bite. Her purpose, once so clear, felt tangled and confused. Her hatred, the very foundation of her existence, was now shaking. The lines between predator and prey, between vengeance and desire, had irrevocably blurred. She had walked into hell to destroy a monster, and instead, she was finding herself bound to him, not by chains, but by a bite she hadn't hated. And that, Lyra knew, was the most terrifying revelation of all. Her undoing had truly begun.

Chapter 18: What the Mirror Reveals

The aftermath of Cassian's bite, the one Lyra hadn't hated, lingered like a potent, intoxicating dream. Her body still hummed with the echoes of pleasure, and her mind felt strangely muddled, the sharp edges of her vengeance blunted by an alarming, bewildering warmth whenever Cassian was near. The hatred that had once been her bedrock felt like shifting sand.

Days bled into nights, a timeless existence within the confines of Cassian's opulent chambers. He continued his peculiar courtship, a dangerous dance of intellect and intimacy. He would spend hours with her, conversing about ancient history, about the stars, about the fragile beauty of mortal life, and the relentless march of immortal time. He offered her books, taught her archaic languages, and even, to her surprise, shared glimpses of his own vast, lonely existence.

The physical contact became more frequent, more profound. Not always bites, but touches – a hand resting on her waist as they walked, his thumb tracing the line of her jaw, a kiss that tasted of power and possession. Each interaction was a subtle erosion of her defenses, a blurring of the lines between captor and… something else she dared not name.

One morning, Lyra awoke to find herself alone in the vast bed. The crimson drapes were drawn, bathing the room in a soft, twilight gloom. The bite mark on her neck throbbed, a dull ache now, but also a constant reminder of the bewildering emotions it had ignited.

She rose, feeling strangely heavy, both physically and emotionally. She walked to the large, ornate mirror that stood in a corner of the room, its silvered surface reflecting the dim light. She looked at her reflection, truly looked, perhaps for the first time since entering Sinful Castle.

The girl staring back was still Lyra Virellan, but subtly, profoundly changed. Her eyes, once burning with a singular, fierce hatred, now held a deeper, more complex light – a mix of defiance, confusion, and a nascent, terrifying vulnerability. The dark circles under her eyes, once a testament to restless nights fueled by vengeance, were now softer, almost gone, replaced by a strange luminescence.

She lifted her hair, examining the bite mark on her neck. It was small, a faint, almost invisible scar, a delicate cluster of tiny punctures. But it was there. A permanent mark. A symbol of his claim. And of her unsettling response to it.

As Lyra gazed at her reflection, a shadow detached itself from the deeper shadows of the room, coalescing into a figure that made her breath hitch. Arkyn.

He stood directly behind her, his reflection appearing in the mirror as if he had always been there, an integral part of the gloom. He was older than Cassian, far older, his features sharper, more ancient, etched with centuries of power and cold calculation. His eyes, the color of frozen twilight, held no warmth, no flicker of amusement, only a profound, chilling emptiness. He wore robes of the darkest gray, intricately embroidered, that seemed to absorb the light around him. His presence was not flamboyant like Cassian's, but insidious, suffocating, a silent weight that pressed down on her.

Lyra's blood ran cold. She hadn't heard him enter. He moved with a supernatural stealth, a ghost among the living. All the warnings from Lorcan, all the secrets from his ledger, crashed down on her. This was the true Minotaur. The one pulling the strings.

"So," Arkyn's voice was a dry, rasping whisper, like sand shifting over stone. It held no emotion, no intonation, yet it vibrated with immense, ancient power. "The specimen thrives. Cassian has… enjoyed his acquisition."

Lyra refused to flinch. She met his gaze in the mirror, her own eyes blazing with a renewed defiance, pushing back against the sudden surge of fear. "Lord Arkyn," she said, her voice steady, despite the tremor in her hands.

"You speak my name," Arkyn murmured, his reflection tilting his head slightly, a purely predatory gesture. "Familiarity is a dangerous thing for a mortal, Lyra Virellan. Especially with those who dwell in the shadows."

"I have learned much in the shadows," Lyra retorted, her gaze unwavering. "More than you perhaps realize."

A faint, almost imperceptible tremor went through Arkyn's reflection. "Indeed. I heard of your… spirited display. And your resilience under Cassian's touch." His cold eyes dropped to the mark on her neck, lingering there with an unnerving intensity. "The Blood of the Unbroken. It is potent. Very potent."

Lyra felt a chill deeper than the castle's ancient stones. He knew. He knew the specific nature of her lineage, and its true purpose in his scheme.

"You manipulate this entire ritual," Lyra accused, her voice low, trembling with a growing anger. "The selections. The forced bonds. It's not for sustenance. It's for something else. Something for your own gain."

Arkyn's lips curved into a cold, chilling smile, devoid of any warmth. "I ensure the future of our kind, little mortal. A future of unparalleled power. And your blood, Lyra, is the final key to unlock that future. A catalyst. A conduit."

He took a step closer, his reflection in the mirror mirroring his movement, his presence expanding, suffocating. Lyra felt a wave of dizziness, a subtle but insidious assault on her mind, trying to overwhelm her senses, to bend her will. It was a manipulative power, an ancient magic she hadn't encountered before.

"You are losing control, Lyra Virellan," Arkyn whispered, his voice resonating directly in her mind, bypassing her ears, a chilling invasion. "The hatred that defines you is fading. Replaced by… desire. For your captor. For the very monster you swore to destroy."

Lyra gasped, her eyes widening. He saw it. He saw the shift within her, the blurring of lines, the unwanted attraction to Cassian. He was playing on her deepest fears, on the betrayal of her own heart.

"No," Lyra choked out, trying to fight back against the mental assault. "My purpose is clear. My vengeance still burns."

Arkyn chuckled, a dry, rattling sound that was more chilling than any roar. "Does it, little mortal? Or does the warmth of his bite, the lure of his touch, begin to overshadow the cold embers of your past? You are changing. Becoming… pliable. The mirror reveals all, Lyra. And it shows me a weapon ready to be wielded. Not by your hand, but by mine."

His ancient eyes glittered with a chilling triumph. "Cassian has softened you. Made you ready. He sees a lover, a challenge. But I see a vessel. The final ingredient in a grand design."

Lyra felt a surge of panic, raw and visceral. He was right. She was changing. The desire was real, a potent fire that threatened to consume her purpose. Arkyn was watching, waiting, manipulating her emotions, her very soul, for his own twisted ends. He had used Cassian's burgeoning affection, her own unexpected response, as a tool in his larger game.

"You are losing control, Lyra," Arkyn repeated, his voice echoing in her mind, growing louder, more insistent. "Of your purpose. Of your heart. Soon, you will lose control of your very self."

Lyra squeezed her eyes shut, fighting against the invasive whisper, against the terrifying truth it contained. The image of Cassian, his golden eyes filled with an unfamiliar tenderness, flashed through her mind, then the image of her parents, their faces blurred by time and grief. The internal conflict was tearing her apart.

When she opened her eyes, Arkyn's reflection was still there, a chilling smile on his lips. He was cold, ancient, utterly ruthless. He didn't care about emotion, about connection, only about power.

"Be warned, Lyra Virellan," Arkyn whispered, his voice resonating one last time in her mind, a final, chilling prophecy. "You are walking a path to your own undoing. And soon, the choice will no longer be yours."

He faded back into the shadows, disappearing as silently as he had appeared, leaving Lyra alone again in the dimly lit room. She stared at her reflection in the mirror, her hands pressed against the cold glass. The girl staring back was indeed changing. Her face was flushed, her eyes wide with a terrifying realization.

Arkyn's words, his chilling assessment of her weakening resolve, echoed in her ears. He had seen the truth in the mirror. He had seen the shift in her heart. And he had warned her.

This wasn't just about vengeance anymore. It was about her very soul. The battle was no longer just external; it was raging within her. The monster beneath Cassian's mask had revealed a hint of humanity, but the monster behind Arkyn's cold eyes was pure, unadulterated evil. And he intended to possess her, not just her blood, but her very essence. Lyra knew she had to regain control, and quickly. Before the mirror revealed her final, terrifying surrender.

Chapter 19: A Dress to Kill In

Arkyn's chilling appearance in the mirror, and his insidious words, had shattered Lyra's fragile composure. The unwanted desire for Cassian, once a subtle hum beneath her skin, now felt like a roaring inferno, threatening to consume her purpose. He had seen it, exploited it, and used it to twist the knife of doubt deeper into her heart. The monster she had come to destroy was not Cassian, but the ancient, calculating being pulling the strings from the shadows. And that monster knew her weaknesses.

The following days were a torment of internal conflict. Lyra tried to reassert control, to cling to the burning embers of her hatred for Arkyn, but the memory of Cassian's gentle touch, the intoxicating rush of his bite, kept intruding, blurring the lines. She avoided his gaze, found excuses to be occupied when he was near, a futile attempt to rebuild the walls around her heart. But he noticed. His golden eyes, sharper than ever, missed nothing.

One evening, as the castle began to stir with the familiar hum of the approaching night, a silent servant entered Lyra's chambers. He carried a heavy, ornate garment bag, its fabric shimmering with an unnatural sheen. He placed it carefully on the chaise lounge, then offered Lyra a small, velvet-covered box.

"Lord Cassian requests your presence at the Ritual of Sacred Blood," the servant murmured, his voice as devoid of emotion as ever. "And he has personally selected your attire for the occasion."

Lyra felt a prickle of unease. *Ritual of Sacred Blood.* The words alone were ominous. This wasn't another dance or a casual gathering. This was clearly a more formal, more significant event. And the fact that Cassian had chosen her dress personally… it felt like another test, another layer of his dangerous game of control.

She dismissed the servant with a nod, her gaze fixed on the garment bag. She walked to it, her heart pounding a strange, anxious rhythm. She unzipped it slowly, revealing the dress within.

It was crimson. A deep, rich, undeniable blood red. The fabric was a heavy, shimmering silk that clung to every curve of the mannequin form it hung on, a stark contrast to the sheer black she had worn before. The neckline plunged daringly, revealing a hint of cleavage, and the back was cut low, almost to her waist. It was designed for utter, undeniable spectacle. It was a dress that screamed for attention, for display, for sacrifice.

Lyra's breath hitched. This wasn't just a dress. This was a statement. A living embodiment of the "Blood Offering" she was meant to be. And the color… it was the color of vengeance, of sacrifice, of the blood she had come to shed.

If I'm going down, I'm going fabulous. The cynical thought, once a source of grim amusement, now felt like a desperate mantra. This dress was designed to make her feel like a lamb dressed for slaughter, to highlight her vulnerability. But Lyra suddenly saw it differently.

This dress wasn't just for him. It was for Arkyn. A challenge. A declaration. If she was to be an offering, she would be an offering they would never forget.

A slow, dangerous smile touched Lyra's lips. She would wear the blood-red dress. She would walk into that ritual, not as a victim, but as a weapon, draped in the very color of their thirst.

She would kill in this dress.

She felt a surge of grim determination. This was her chance. Her purpose, which Arkyn had tried so desperately to blur, now shone with renewed clarity. Cassian's attachment, his confusing tenderness, could be a weakness for her, yes. But it could also be a shield, a blind spot for Arkyn. She would use it. She would use everything.

Lyra carefully laid out the dress. The plunging neckline was a risk, but the very boldness of it could be a distraction. She started to prepare herself, her movements deliberate, precise. She braided her long, dark hair into an intricate coil at the nape of her neck, exposing the faint bite marks, a silent testament to Cassian's claim. She applied a bold, crimson lipstick, matching the dress, a stark contrast to her pale skin.

Her eyes, now blazing with a cold, renewed resolve, seemed to mirror the fiery color of the gown.

She then reached for the small, concealed dagger. This dress, unlike the black silk, would not easily hide it. But Lyra had anticipated this. She found a delicate silver garter, designed to hold a tiny vial of perfume, and repurposed it. The dagger, small and impossibly sharp, nestled perfectly inside, hidden by the flowing silk of the skirt, but easily accessible if she needed it. A silent, deadly promise.

She looked at herself in the mirror, clad in the blood-red gown. She looked beautiful, undeniably so. And utterly lethal.

I am not a sacrifice. I am a storm.

A faint knock on the door, lighter this time. It wasn't the servant. It was Cassian. Lyra felt a flutter in her stomach, a nervous excitement that had nothing to do with fear. This was her moment.

She opened the door. Cassian stood there, clad in formal, dark robes, his golden eyes sweeping over her, taking in the full effect of the crimson dress. His gaze lingered on the plunging neckline, on the bare skin of her back, on the bold splash of red at her lips. His eyes darkened, a potent mixture of hunger and possessive satisfaction.

"Remarkable," he murmured, his voice husky, a low, appreciative growl. "Truly… breathtaking, Lyra Virellan." He took a step closer, his hand reaching out, his fingers lightly tracing the line of her collarbone, just above the healing bite mark. "The color suits you. It screams… passion. And power."

Lyra met his gaze, a subtle, challenging smile on her lips. "And blood, Lord Cassian," she added softly, her voice holding a knowing edge. "Don't forget the blood."

His lips curved into a slow, predatory smile. "Never. Especially not yours." He leaned in, his lips brushing against her ear. "Tonight, Lyra, is a night of… profound exchange. And you, my little defiant one, will be at its very heart."

Lyra felt a shiver run down her spine, not from fear, but from the chilling double meaning of his words. She knew what he meant by "profound exchange" – a deeper merging of blood, perhaps a formal claiming. But she also knew Arkyn's true agenda. This ritual was about more than just a vampire taking a mortal as his own. It was about stealing power.

"I am ready," Lyra stated, her voice firm, unwavering. She met his gaze, her eyes blazing with a renewed sense of purpose. "For whatever exchanges the night holds."

Cassian's golden eyes gleamed, a flicker of genuine surprise at her bold resolve. He offered her his arm. Lyra took it, her hand resting lightly on his forearm. The touch was familiar now, a strange blend of comfort and danger.

As they walked through the opulent corridors, Lyra felt the weight of the dagger against her thigh, a silent, deadly promise. She had chosen this dress, not for him, but for herself. To be seen. To be feared. And tonight, at the Ritual of Sacred Blood, she would unleash the storm. Her heart still wrestled with the bewildering emotions for Cassian, but her purpose, sharpened by Arkyn's cruel manipulation, was clearer than ever. She was here to kill. And she would do it in a dress designed for just that. A dress to kill in.

Chapter 20: Before the Blade Strikes

The Ritual of Sacred Blood was not a ball; it was a ceremony, ancient and chilling. The grand hall, usually bathed in warm light, was now lit by hundreds of black candles, their flickering flames casting dancing shadows that made the vampire faces seem even more predatory, their eyes gleaming with an eerie intensity. The air was thick with the scent of burning incense, something musky, and the unmistakable, metallic tang of blood, richer and more potent than before.

Lyra walked beside Cassian, draped in the crimson silk dress that felt less like a gown and more like a shroud. Every eye in the room was on them, their gazes a tangible weight on her skin. She felt like a figure in a macabre tableau, a central piece in a ritual whose true purpose only a chilling few understood. Cassian's hand rested possessively at the small of her back, his presence a constant, powerful hum beside her. He exuded an aura of calm, yet Lyra could feel the subtle tension beneath his control, the coiled power waiting to be unleashed.

She scanned the room, her gaze sweeping over the assembled vampire lords. Lorcan stood slightly apart from the others, his twilight eyes watching her, a flicker of warning in their depths. And then, Lyra saw him. Arkyn.

He stood on a raised dais at the far end of the hall, not with the other High Lords, but elevated, almost enthroned. He was cloaked in robes even darker than before, seemingly absorbing the light around him, making him appear as if he was carved from pure shadow. His ancient face was impassive, his eyes, like chips of frozen starlight, held no discernible emotion, yet Lyra felt their chilling weight. He was the puppet master, the architect of her pain, the true monster. The dagger, concealed against her thigh, felt like a burning promise. Tonight, she would strike.

The ritual began. An ancient, gaunt vampire, acting as the high priest, began to chant in a guttural, arcane language Lyra didn't understand, but whose meaning resonated with a chilling power. He spoke of ancient bloodlines, of power, of sacrifice, and of a grand destiny for the vampire kind.

Lyra forced herself to remain outwardly calm, her expression serene, almost bored, while her mind raced. This was her opportunity. During the climax of the ritual, when all eyes would be on the high priest, on the sacrifice, she would make her move. She would get close enough to Cassian, close enough to pierce his immortal heart. It was a risky, desperate plan, but the only one she had. And if she could take him down, perhaps she could expose Arkyn. Or at least disrupt his sinister ritual.

As the chanting intensified, the high priest moved to a large, black stone altar in the center of the dais. On it rested an ornate, silver chalice, intricately carved with symbols of blood and power. The offering, Lyra knew, would come forward, and her blood would be presented.

Cassian tightened his grip on her back. "Almost time, little mortal," he whispered, his voice a low, possessive murmur. "Prepare yourself for the merging."

Lyra felt a jolt. *The merging.* Lorcan's words about Arkyn seeking to control what he could not break, about her blood being the "final key," echoed ominously in her mind. This was not just about Cassian claiming her. This was about Arkyn's ritual, his attempt to extract and weaponize the Blood of the Unbroken.

She met Cassian's gaze, her eyes holding a deceptive softness. She would play her part, lull him into a false sense of security. And then, she would strike.

The high priest finished his chant, his voice rising to a crescendo. He raised his arms, and a blinding flash of dark energy erupted from the altar, momentarily illuminating the entire hall. The air thrummed with a potent, ancient magic.

"Let the vessels be presented!" the high priest boomed, his voice echoing.

Lyra felt Cassian's hand move from her back, drawing her forward. She walked towards the dais, her steps measured, deliberate. She could feel Arkyn's cold, unwavering gaze on her, observing every subtle movement.

She ascended the steps to the dais, standing beside Cassian, facing the high priest and, beyond him, Arkyn. She could feel the dagger, a cold weight against her thigh, a silent promise of defiance. Her heart pounded a frantic rhythm against her ribs. This was it. The moment.

The high priest began a new chant, this one directed at Lyra. Cassian moved closer, his hand reaching out for hers, lacing their fingers together. His golden eyes, filled with a mixture of raw desire and possessive pride, met hers. He was completely focused on her, on the ritual, oblivious to the storm brewing beneath her calm exterior.

Lyra's gaze flickered to Arkyn. His eyes were fixed on her, cold and triumphant. He knew. He knew about her blood, about the power he intended to steal. And he had underestimated her.

This was her chance. Her hand, intertwined with Cassian's, was close enough. The dagger was inches away, concealed beneath the flowing crimson silk. She tightened her grip on his hand, preparing to strike. Her heart hammered, the blood rushing in her ears.

She pulled the dagger free, her movement swift, fluid, hidden by the folds of her dress and the sheer speed of her action. The cold steel felt familiar, a true extension of her will. She brought it up, aiming for his heart, the vulnerable spot she had researched, the very core of his immortal being.

Her arm was mid-arc, the blade glinting ominously in the black candlelight, poised to plunge into Cassian's chest. Her eyes were fixed on his heart, burning with a fierce, singular purpose. This was for her family. For their blood. For vengeance.

Just as the blade was about to strike, as her arm tensed for the final, fatal thrust, Cassian moved. Not to block, not to defend. He leaned in, his lips brushing against her ear, his voice a low, unexpected whisper that cut through the roaring blood in her ears, shattering her focus, freezing her.

"I remember your mother."

The words hit Lyra like a physical blow. The dagger faltered, hovering inches from his chest. Her arm trembled, her eyes widening in stunned disbelief. Her mother. He remembered her. He had seen her. It was a twist she had never anticipated, a revelation that shook her to her core, unraveling years of carefully constructed hatred in a single, devastating whisper. The blade, poised for death, froze in mid-air, caught between vengeance and an unbearable, mind-shattering question.

Chapter 21: The Truth Buried in Blood

The blade, inches from Cassian's chest, trembled in Lyra's hand. His words, "I remember your mother," echoed in the thrumming silence of the hall, a devastating blow that shattered her focus, her resolve, and the very foundation of her hatred. Her arm, once so steady, now shook uncontrollably.

Cassian's golden eyes, no longer gleaming with possessive triumph, now held a profound, unsettling sadness as he looked at her. He saw her shock, her confusion, the raw pain tearing through her. He didn't move, didn't flinch. He simply waited, his gaze locked with hers, allowing her the space to process the impossible truth he had just whispered.

The high priest, startled by the sudden stillness, by the halted ritual, looked on with confusion. The other vampire lords, sensing the profound shift in the air, murmured uneasily, their eyes darting between Lyra, the poised blade, and Cassian's unreadable face. Arkyn, however, remained impassive on his dais, his ancient eyes fixed on the scene, a subtle, almost imperceptible flicker of concern in their depths.

Lyra's breath hitched. Her mother. It was impossible. The monster who had orchestrated her family's demise, the one whose blood she swore to shed, could not possibly *remember* her mother with such a tone, such a look in his eyes.

"What... what do you mean?" Lyra choked out, her voice barely a whisper, raw with a desperate need for understanding. The dagger, still clutched in her trembling hand, felt impossibly heavy.

Cassian's gaze never left hers. His lips, stained faintly with the lingering memory of her blood, curved into a bitter, melancholic smile. "She was... brave," he murmured, his voice low, filled with an ancient weariness. "Fierce. And loyal to a fault. Even in defiance."

He took her trembling hand, his fingers gently closing over hers, guiding the blade, not away, but slightly to the side, away from his heart, towards the space between them. It was a gesture of profound trust, or perhaps, a terrifying challenge.

"She refused to yield," he continued, his voice a low, resonant rumble that seemed to reverberate through her very bones. "Even when Arkyn demanded her blood for his ritual. She chose to fight."

Lyra's eyes widened, a sudden, horrifying clarity dawning on her. Arkyn. Not Cassian. It was Arkyn, the puppet master, the one pulling the strings, who had truly orchestrated her family's destruction. Cassian had merely been... a witness. Or, perhaps, something more.

"Arkyn?" Lyra whispered, the name a bitter taste on her tongue.

Cassian nodded slowly, his golden eyes filled with a pain that seemed to stretch across centuries. "He sought to break your bloodline, Lyra. To claim the 'Unbroken' essence. Your family... they resisted his first attempts. Your father fought with the ferocity of a lion. Your mother... she shielded you. She bought you time."

He leaned in closer, his voice dropping to an urgent whisper, meant only for her ears, overriding the murmurs of the other vampires, the confusion of the high priest. "I was there, Lyra. Not as their killer, but as... a participant in a battle I did not fully understand. I was sent to... ensure compliance. But when Arkyn's power threatened to consume everything... I shielded you. I saw your mother's strength. I saw her sacrifice. And I recognized... something unique in you. Something that Arkyn craves. And something I... could not allow him to fully claim."

Lyra stared at him, breathless, her mind reeling. The narrative of her life, the hatred that had defined her, was crumbling into dust. Cassian, the monster she sought to kill, was not the monster of her past. He had been there, yes. But he had not been the killer. He had, impossibly, *saved* her.

The dagger clattered from her numb fingers, hitting the stone dais with a sharp, echoing clang that cut through the silence of the hall. The sound was deafening, a testament to her shattered world.

The high priest, visibly agitated, spoke, "Lord Cassian, the ritual must continue! The offering is... compromised!"

Cassian ignored him. His gaze was fixed on Lyra, a profound sadness in his golden eyes. "The lie has festered for too long," he murmured, his voice laced with regret. "Arkyn allowed you to believe it. He nurtured your hatred, knowing it would bring you back here. To him."

Lyra looked past Cassian, her gaze now fixed on Arkyn on the dais. The ancient vampire's impassive face finally showed a flicker of something: a cold, calculating triumph, mixed with a fleeting concern that his carefully constructed plan was now exposed. He had manipulated her. He had fed her vengeance, knowing it would lead her, a potent vessel of the "Unbroken Blood," directly into his grasp. He had used Cassian as a decoy, a villain in her eyes, while he prepared his final, ultimate move.

All the pieces clicked into place: Lorcan's cryptic warnings, the secrets in his ledgers about Arkyn's manipulations, the "Blood of the Unbroken," the true purpose of the selections. It wasn't about sating hunger. It was about power. And Lyra was the ultimate prize.

A wave of overwhelming fury, colder and more potent than anything she had felt before, washed over Lyra. Not for Cassian, but for Arkyn. For the decades of manipulation, for the twisted game, for using her grief, her very soul, as a pawn in his ancient, monstrous scheme.

"He is the one," Lyra whispered, her voice raw with a newfound, terrifying clarity. She looked at Cassian, her eyes blazing with a fierce, terrible light. "He is the monster."

Cassian nodded slowly, his hand still holding hers, a silent pact forged in the shattered remnants of her vengeance. "Indeed. And he seeks to complete what he began all those years ago. With your blood. With your very essence." He squeezed her hand, his golden eyes holding a promise of alliance. "But not if I have anything to say about it."

The truth, buried in blood and lies for so long, had finally been unearthed. And Lyra, stripped of her convenient enemy, now faced the true, ancient evil that had haunted her life. The blade had not struck Cassian, but it was now poised to strike at the heart of the true master of Sinful Castle. The ritual, meant to bind her, had just set her free. Free to fight the real war.

Chapter 22: A Thirst Older Than Vengeance

The air in the grand hall crackled, not with the oppressive magic of the ritual, but with the raw tension of exposed truths. Lyra stood beside Cassian, her former enemy, the man she had come to kill, now her unlikely ally. The high priest and the assembled vampire lords murmured, their faces a mixture of confusion and unease. Arkyn, however, remained impassive on his dais, his ancient eyes betraying nothing but a faint, chilling satisfaction. He had anticipated this. He had planned for this.

Lyra's gaze, no longer clouded by the fog of engineered hatred, burned with a cold, clear fury directed solely at Arkyn. He was the puppeteer, the true architect of her family's demise, the one who sought to twist her blood for his own monstrous ambition. Vengeance, once a personal mission, now encompassed a larger, more terrifying scope.

Cassian's hand, still holding hers, tightened imperceptibly. His golden eyes, usually alight with a predatory amusement, were now filled with a grim resolve as he met Arkyn's gaze across the hall. The silent communication between them was palpable: a declaration of war.

"This 'ritual of sacred blood'," Lyra stated, her voice clear and strong, cutting through the murmurs, "is a lie. A deception. It is not about honor or tradition. It is about a thirst for power older than vengeance itself. Lord Arkyn."

Her accusation, spoken so plainly, caused a ripple of shocked gasps among the assembled vampires. Many looked at Arkyn, then back at Lyra, their faces a mixture of disbelief and nascent suspicion. Arkyn's face remained a mask, but a subtle tremor ran through the air around him, a flicker of ancient power disturbed.

"Insolent mortal!" the granite-faced High Lord boomed, attempting to restore order, his voice filled with outrage. "How dare you accuse a Lord of the Ancient Houses, the very foundation of our existence!"

"I dare," Lyra retorted, her eyes blazing, "because the truth has been buried long enough. Lord Arkyn seeks to harness the essence of the 'Blood of the Unbroken' – my bloodline – to fuel his own dark magic, to elevate himself to an unimaginable power." She looked around the hall, addressing the bewildered vampires directly. "This 'selection' of offerings? It is nothing more than a series of twisted experiments, searching for the perfect vessel, the perfect catalyst for his ultimate design."

A cacophony of whispers erupted. The vampires exchanged uneasy glances. Some scoffed, but many looked truly alarmed. The idea of Arkyn manipulating such sacred rituals for personal gain was a profound violation of their ancient traditions.

Arkyn finally moved. He slowly rose from his elevated position, his dark robes seeming to swallow the light. He descended the steps, his movements silent, graceful, terrifyingly deliberate. Every eye followed him. His ancient eyes, devoid of warmth, fixed on Lyra with a chilling intensity.

"A rather dramatic tale, little mortal," Arkyn's voice rasped, a dry, chilling whisper that carried effortlessly across the hall, drawing all attention. "Born of fear, no doubt. The mind plays tricks when confronted with the inevitable."

"Fear?" Lyra scoffed, a bitter laugh escaping her. "I know true fear, Lord Arkyn. And it is not of death. It is of a monster who manipulates lives, twists truths, and sacrifices innocents for his own twisted ambition." She took a step forward, pulling Cassian with her, revealing the faint mark on her neck. "Cassian did not kill my family. He saved me. You orchestrated their destruction. You nurtured my hatred, knowing it would lead me back here, into your grasp."

A collective gasp swept through the hall. The accusation, so raw, so direct, sent shockwaves through the vampire court. Cassian, beside Lyra, remained silent, his grip on her hand firm, a silent testament to her words.

Arkyn stopped a few feet from them, his presence radiating a cold, ancient power that made the air shimmer. "A convenient narrative, I daresay," he stated, his voice still unnervingly calm. "To absolve your newfound… fascination. But mortal emotions are fleeting. And truth… is carved in history. A history you know nothing of."

"I know enough," Lyra countered, her voice unwavering. "I know you seek my blood, the 'Blood of the Unbroken,' because it resists your ancient magic. You want to twist it, to enslave it, to use it as a conduit for a power that should never be awakened." She met his cold gaze, her eyes blazing. "You manipulated this entire selection process, experimenting with the blood of countless women, all to find the perfect vessel for your monstrous goal."

Suddenly, Lorcan stepped forward from the High Lords' dais. His twilight eyes, usually so impassive, now held a deep, ancient sorrow, mixed with a resolute fire.

"She speaks the truth," Lorcan's voice resonated, a calm, clear baritone that cut through the agitated whispers. "Arkyn has long sought to corrupt the ancient blood-rites. His thirst is not for sustenance, but for absolute dominion. He manipulates the currents of power, seeking to bind not just mortals, but our very kind, to his will." He looked at the assembled vampires, his gaze sweeping over their faces. "He desires a throne, not of our choosing, but of his own creation. Fueled by enslaved souls and stolen power."

A stunned silence descended upon the hall. Lorcan's words, spoken by one of their own, one of the most respected and ancient, carried immense weight. The murmurs turned into agitated whispers, then open cries of disbelief and anger. The carefully constructed façade of the ritual, of Arkyn's benevolent leadership, was crumbling.

Arkyn's face, for the first time, lost its impassive mask. His eyes, usually so cold, now blazed with a terrifying, ancient fury. A low, guttural snarl escaped him, a sound of pure, unadulterated rage. He had been exposed. His deepest secrets, laid bare by the most unexpected of allies – a human girl and his quiet, watchful brother.

"Betrayal!" Arkyn roared, his voice now amplified by raw, uncontrolled power, vibrating through the hall, shaking the very foundations of the castle. Dark energy crackled around him, swirling like an ominous storm. "You dare to challenge me, Lorcan? You dare to align with a mortal whose blood I have claimed?"

"I align with truth, brother," Lorcan countered, his voice steady despite the surge of Arkyn's power. "And with what little honor remains in this fractured court."

Cassian stepped fully in front of Lyra, shielding her, his body a formidable wall between her and Arkyn's unleashed fury.

His golden eyes blazed with a fierce, protective light, mirroring the rage in Arkyn's.

"Your games are over, Arkyn," Cassian growled, his voice deep and resonant with barely contained power. "The Thirst for dominance has consumed you. And it ends tonight."

Arkyn's gaze, now filled with venomous hatred, flickered from Lorcan to Cassian, and finally, settled on Lyra, a chilling promise of retribution in their depths. "This is not over," he snarled, his voice trembling with fury. "You have unearthed truths, little mortal, but you have only hastened your own destruction. The blood calls. And I will claim it. All of it."

With a final, terrifying glare, Arkyn's form dissolved into a swirling vortex of shadows, vanishing from the dais, leaving behind a lingering scent of ozone and ancient malice. The hall was plunged into a stunned silence, broken only by the rapid breathing of the assembled vampires and the faint, unsettling hum of residual power.

Lyra stood, gripping Cassian's hand, her body trembling not from fear, but from the sheer magnitude of the confrontation, the undeniable truth that had just been laid bare. Arkyn was the true monster. He had been manipulating everything from the shadows, his thirst for power far older and more insidious than any vengeance she had ever conceived. The battle had just begun.

Chapter 23: Kiss Before Betrayal

The echoing silence in the grand hall was more deafening than any scream. Arkyn had vanished, leaving behind a tangible void and a simmering unease among the assembled vampires. His raw fury, his exposed ambition, had shaken the very foundations of their ancient court. Whispers erupted once more, louder, more frantic than before, as the truth of his manipulations sank in.

Lyra stood beside Cassian, her hand still clutched in his, the phantom weight of the dagger she had almost plunged into his heart now a chilling memory. The confusion and hatred she'd felt for him had evaporated, replaced by a profound sense of alliance, and something deeper, something she still refused to name. He had saved her, not just from Arkyn's direct grasp, but from a lifetime of fighting the wrong enemy.

Cassian's golden eyes, still blazing with the aftermath of his confrontation with Arkyn, swept over the startled faces of the other vampire lords. His grip on Lyra's hand tightened, a silent declaration of ownership and protection.

"The ritual is concluded," Cassian's voice boomed, cutting through the murmurs, resonating with a power that commanded attention. "Lord Arkyn has revealed his true nature. The ancient laws have been violated. His reign of manipulation ends tonight."

The high priest, the granite-faced Lord, looked torn, his gaze flickering between the empty dais where Arkyn had stood and the formidable figure of Cassian. "Lord Cassian," he began, his voice hesitant, "this is… unprecedented. We must convene the Council. Deliberate on the accusations…"

"Deliberation is for cowards and the complicit," Cassian snarled, his lips curving into a predatory smile that held no humor. "The truth has been laid bare. He seeks to enslave our kind, to corrupt our very essence. There is no debate. There is only war." His eyes fixed on the vampire lords, challenging them. "Choose your side. Now."

A tense silence fell. The other vampire lords exchanged uncertain glances. Arkyn's power was ancient and terrifying, but Cassian's raw strength and newfound clarity, backed by Lorcan's surprising revelation, held a different kind of undeniable force.

Lyra felt a surge of adrenaline. This was it. The moment of reckoning. The shifting of allegiances. Her revelation, coupled with Lorcan's testimony, had created the chaos needed to dismantle Arkyn's control.

Lorcan, who had returned to his place among the High Lords, stepped forward once more. His twilight eyes, usually so composed, now held a fierce, determined light. "Brother Cassian speaks the truth," he affirmed, his voice steady and resonant. "Arkyn has betrayed us all. He has used the very blood of our lineage for his dark experiments. He must be stopped."

Lorcan's words, from a trusted elder, swayed many. A few of the younger, more impressionable vampires openly declared their allegiance to Cassian. Others, older and more cautious, remained hesitant, their faces grim. The court was divided, but Arkyn's power was weakened.

Cassian turned his head, his golden eyes meeting Lyra's. The raw possessiveness was still there, but now it was tinged with something else: a silent question, a shared understanding of the monumental choice that lay before them.

"Lyra," he murmured, his voice low, meant only for her. "The truth has been revealed. You now know who the true enemy is. The one who truly destroyed your family. The one who seeks to claim you, not for blood, but for power. You have a choice."

Lyra's heart pounded. The choice. It was stark, terrifyingly clear, and yet impossibly complex.

Option 1: Trust Cassian. Align herself with him. Fight alongside the monster who had unknowingly saved her, to dismantle Arkyn's system, and perhaps, find a new purpose. This meant letting go of the ingrained hatred, embracing the bewildering connection, and stepping into an unknown future. It meant facing the ultimate betrayal of her past self, of her singular mission of vengeance.

Option 2: Continue her original plan. Stick to her vengeance. Kill Cassian here, now, in the chaos, as a symbol of defiance against *all* vampires, then try to find a way to strike at Arkyn herself, perhaps sacrificing herself in the process. This path offered a clean, if bloody, resolution to her personal hatred, a return to the familiar, albeit devastating, purpose that had defined her. It meant rejecting the confusing, unwanted feelings for Cassian, and embracing isolation.

Her gaze swept over the hall. The bewildered faces of the other offerings, the fragile hope in their eyes. Lorcan, a silent ally, watching her with a plea in his gaze. Arkyn, a shadow, already gone, but his chilling presence still palpable. And Cassian, standing beside her, offering her a hand, a choice she never thought she'd have.

This was not just about her vengeance. This was about the other girls. About the ancient ritual. About breaking a tyrannical system. About choosing a future, not just dwelling in the past.

Lyra looked at Cassian, his golden eyes earnest, waiting. The beast she had come to kill had revealed a deeper truth, a surprising capacity for something akin to honor, even devotion. The kiss she had almost given him with a blade, now felt like a test, a brutal, unforeseen turning point.

She took a deep breath, the decision solidifying in her heart. The hatred was gone, replaced by a cold, righteous fury against Arkyn. And the bewildering connection with Cassian was undeniably real. She chose the future. She chose the fight. She chose… him.

"I choose to fight the true monster," Lyra declared, her voice clear and strong, resonating through the hall, solidifying her choice. She looked directly at Cassian, her eyes blazing with a fierce, unwavering resolve. "I choose... to stand with you. Against him."

A wave of relief, quickly masked by a grim satisfaction, washed over Cassian's face. His grip on her hand tightened, a silent confirmation of their alliance.

He leaned in, his lips brushing against hers, a soft, deliberate touch. It wasn't the hungry, possessive kiss of his bite, but something deeper, more meaningful. A kiss of alliance. A kiss of shared purpose. A kiss before a betrayal, not of him, but of the very path she had walked for so long.

"Then the battle begins," Cassian murmured against her lips, his voice husky. "And together, Lyra Virellan, we shall bring this castle, and Arkyn's reign, to its knees."

Lyra met his gaze, a fierce, determined light in her eyes. The choice was made. The hatred for Arkyn burned, hotter and clearer than ever. And the unexpected connection with Cassian, once a torment, was now a perplexing, yet potent, strength. The path to her undoing, ironically, had just become the path to her true purpose. The real war had truly begun.

Chapter 24: Marked by Fire, Not Fangs

The decision, once agonizing, now felt clear, a burning ember of purpose in Lyra's heart. She had chosen to fight not just for herself, but for the other offerings, for the future of a world free from Arkyn's chilling manipulation. Cassian stood beside her, his presence a formidable anchor in the swirling chaos of the hall. Their alliance, forged in blood and newfound trust, was a silent declaration of war against the ancient, insidious evil.

The stunned silence in the hall shattered as Cassian's command rang out: "Secure the castle! Alert the guard. Lord Arkyn is a traitor to the Ancient Houses. He seeks to corrupt our very essence. His rule ends tonight!"

His words ignited a frenzy of activity. Vampire guards, initially bewildered, now moved with swift precision, following Cassian's orders. The High Lords, still reeling from the revelations, began to break into agitated discussions, some siding with Cassian, others still hesitant, their loyalty to Arkyn deeply ingrained.

Lyra's gaze swept over the remaining offerings, still huddled in fear. Their eyes, wide and bewildered, looked to her, to Cassian, for answers, for hope. She wouldn't abandon them. They were integral to Arkyn's ritual, his "experiments." Freeing them was paramount.

"The offerings!" Lyra called out, her voice clear and strong, cutting through the rising clamor. "They are not sacrifices. They are prisoners! They must be freed!"

Cassian, his golden eyes blazing with a fierce resolve, nodded. "Lorcan," he commanded, his voice sharp. "Gather those who are loyal. Ensure the offerings are protected. And secure the ceremonial chambers. Do not let Arkyn return to them!"

Lorcan, already moving, inclined his head. "As you command, brother. The labyrinth is deep. We will need fire to flush out his shadows." He shot a meaningful glance at Lyra, a silent acknowledgment of her role, and the danger they faced.

The castle plunged into controlled chaos. Loyal guards, identifiable by a different crest on their armor, began to round up those who remained hesitant or openly hostile. Shouts echoed through the ancient halls, interspersed with the clash of distant skirmishes. The elegant ball was now a battlefield.

Lyra grabbed Cassian's arm, her voice urgent. "Arkyn won't abandon his plan. He'll retreat to his hidden chambers, to the heart of the ritual. We need to cut him off. And we need to free the girls."

"He will be expecting us," Cassian replied, his jaw tight. "He knows every shadow in this castle."

"Then we make new shadows," Lyra said, her eyes flashing with a dangerous light. "And we make them burn." Her gaze swept to a towering, ornate tapestry depicting an ancient vampire battle, hanging near a grand staircase. The fabric was old, dry, and highly flammable. And just beneath it, a forgotten torch sconce.

Cassian followed her gaze, a slow, predatory smile spreading across his lips. He understood. "A reckless strategy, little mortal," he murmured, a glint of approval in his golden eyes. "But fitting."

"If I'm going down," Lyra whispered, her lips curving into a grim, determined smile, "I'm going fabulous. And I'm taking the whole damn castle with me."

With a nod from Cassian, she moved. Swiftly, silently, she ran to the torch sconce. Her fingers, nimble and accustomed to clandestine work, easily retrieved the smoldering torch. Its flame flickered, casting eerie shadows on her determined face.

She brought the torch to the edge of the ancient tapestry. The dry fabric caught instantly, a hungry lick of flame devouring the aged threads. The fire spread rapidly, climbing the tapestry, sending sparks showering into the air.

A collective gasp went through the hall. Some vampires cried out in alarm, others in outrage. The heat intensified, and the crackle of burning fabric filled the air, replacing the sounds of battle.

"Fire!" someone screamed. "The castle is burning!"

Panic erupted. The other offerings, who had been huddled in fear, suddenly found a desperate surge of energy. Seeing Lyra, a mortal, ignite such a defiant blaze, instilled in them a frantic hope.

"Follow me!" Lyra yelled, her voice cutting through the din, amplified by adrenaline. She waved the burning torch, its flame licking upwards. "The passages below! There's a way out!"

Cassian, now fully engaged in the ensuing chaos, turned to her, his eyes blazing with a mixture of possessive admiration and urgent command. "Lyra, run! The hidden passages. Lorcan will guide them!"

He drew a gleaming, ancient sword from a scabbard held by a loyal guard, its blade shimmering with dark power. He moved towards the approaching threats, a formidable force, ready to engage. "Go! I will hold them off!"

Lyra hesitated for a split second, her gaze fixed on him. The risk was immense. But she trusted him. She had to.

She turned to the terrified offerings. "Follow me! Now! This way!" She led them towards a concealed door she knew from Lorcan's map, located behind another tapestry, away from the main conflict.

The fire spread, casting an ominous, flickering glow throughout the hall. Smoke began to curl towards the high ceilings, creating a disorienting haze. The screams of confused vampires, the shouts of loyalists, and the crackle of flames filled the air.

Lyra reached the hidden door. It was bolted from the inside. With a desperate surge of strength, she slammed her shoulder against it, then again, her muscles screaming with effort. The wood groaned, and the ancient bolt finally gave way.

She pushed the door open, revealing a dark, narrow passage. "Go! Now! Tell them Lyra sent you! Lorcan will meet you!" she urged the terrified girls, pushing them through the opening. They stumbled, but their desperation fueled them, and they scrambled into the darkness.

Just as the last girl disappeared into the passage, a massive, shadowy figure emerged from the smoke, lunging towards Lyra. It was a High Lord, his face contorted with rage, his eyes burning with hatred. He saw her, the mortal who had dared to ignite his sacred castle.

Before he could reach her, Cassian appeared, a blur of dark vengeance. His sword flashed, a silver streak in the firelight. The High Lord roared, but Cassian was faster, more precise, fueled by a protective fury. He engaged the vampire in a brutal, swift exchange, their blades clashing with a metallic shriek.

Lyra spared one last glance at the battle, at Cassian fighting fiercely to hold the line, then she turned and slipped into the hidden passage, closing the door behind her, plunging into the echoing darkness.

She was marked by fire now, not just by fangs. The flames roared behind her, a defiant symbol of destruction and a terrifying act of liberation. The castle was collapsing around her, both physically and figuratively. But for the first time since she had arrived, Lyra felt a flicker of true hope. The undoing had begun. And she, the mortal weapon, was at its fiery heart.

Chapter 25: The Undoing Begins

The hidden passage Lyra had slipped into was a winding, treacherous tunnel, echoing with the distant roar of flames and the muffled sounds of battle from above. The air was thick with dust and the acrid scent of smoke, but Lyra pressed on, driven by a fierce determination. The map from Lorcan's study was a vital guide, its faded lines now a lifeline in the inky blackness.

She moved with urgency, knowing every second counted. Cassian was holding the line, but he couldn't do it forever. And Arkyn, the true puppet master, was still at large, likely retreating to his deepest, most protected sanctums. Lyra's goal was clear: rendezvous with the other offerings, guide them to safety, and then find a way to cut off Arkyn before he could complete his twisted ritual.

The passage eventually opened into a vast, subterranean cavern. It was darker here, colder, the air heavy with ancient magic. The cavern branched into several smaller tunnels, but Lyra recognized the symbols carved into the rough stone walls – the same esoteric markings she'd seen in Lorcan's ledgers, marking ceremonial sites. Arkyn's domain.

Just as Lyra emerged into the cavern, a soft gasp of relief echoed from the shadows. The other offerings. They were here, huddled together, their faces pale with terror, their eyes wide and desperate. Lorcan stood among them, his presence a quiet anchor in the surrounding chaos, his twilight eyes fixed on Lyra.

"Lyra!" one of the girls, the terrified blonde from the first selection, whimpered, rushing forward to cling to her. Lyra wrapped an arm around her, offering what little comfort she could.

"Are you all safe?" Lyra asked, her voice firm, taking charge.

Lorcan nodded. "Most are here. A few scattered in the panic, but we guided these ones to the rendezvous point." He looked at Lyra, a hint of admiration in his gaze. "The fire was… effective. It created the necessary distraction."

"It was a calculated risk," Lyra stated, her eyes sweeping over the frightened faces of the offerings. They were weak, traumatized, but alive. And they were her responsibility now.

Suddenly, a familiar, chilling voice resonated through the cavern, echoing from the darkest, deepest tunnel ahead. It was dry, rasping, filled with ancient menace. Arkyn.

"So," his voice echoed, calm and chillingly amused. "The little mortal who ignites fires. And the brother who betrays. How… touching."

Lyra's blood ran cold. He was here. And he knew. He knew about her, about Lorcan, about the escape.

Arkyn emerged from the tunnel, not with a flourish, but with an ominous stillness. He was cloaked in robes even darker than before, seemingly absorbing all light, his form a silhouette against the faint glow from the main castle above. His ancient eyes, like chips of frozen starlight, fixed directly on Lyra, a chilling triumph in their depths. He was unscathed, unhurried, utterly confident.

"You have been… busy, Lyra Virellan," Arkyn purred, his voice resonating directly in her mind, bypassing her ears, a chilling invasion. "Unearthing secrets. Stirring rebellion. Even setting fires. All quite commendable for a fragile mortal."

"Your reign of manipulation ends tonight, Arkyn," Lyra countered, her voice ringing with defiance, pushing back against his mental assault. She stepped forward, placing herself between Arkyn and the terrified offerings.

He chuckled, a dry, rattling sound. "Does it? Or does it merely begin anew? You have served your purpose, Lyra. You have confirmed the potency of your blood. The 'Blood of the Unbroken' is indeed the catalyst I sought. And now, you are mine."

Lyra felt a surge of cold fury. "Ownership is so last century, Lord Arkyn," she spat, her voice laced with venom. "I am no one's property. And my blood, my essence, will never be yours to corrupt."

Arkyn's eyes narrowed, a flicker of irritation in their depths. "Such tiresome defiance. But easily overcome. Cassian has prepared you. He has softened your resolve. He has awakened the desire within you. He sees a queen. But I see… a tool. A weapon to be wielded. A vessel to be filled."

He took a step closer, his presence radiating an immense, suffocating power that made the air heavy, pressing down on Lyra. The frightened offerings whimpered, shrinking back behind Lorcan.

"Tonight, Lyra Virellan," Arkyn declared, his voice deepening, vibrating with raw, ancient magic, "you will complete the ritual. Not as Cassian's chosen, but as my ultimate vessel. You will be assimilated. Transformed. You will bear the essence of the Unbroken, merged with ancient power, for my dominion. You will be… *possessed*."

He extended a hand, his long, skeletal fingers reaching for her, not to touch, but to envelop her in a field of chilling power. Lyra felt a terrifying pull, an invisible force trying to draw her towards him, to claim her. Her blood hummed in protest, fighting against the invasive magic.

"No!" Lyra screamed, fighting against the unseen force. She felt her muscles strain, her body tremble as she resisted.

Lorcan suddenly stepped forward, his body radiating a quiet, yet potent, energy. He placed a protective hand on Lyra's shoulder, attempting to counter Arkyn's power. "You will not touch her, brother!" he growled, his voice unusually fierce.

Arkyn merely scoffed, a chilling sneer twisting his ancient features. "You are weak, Lorcan. You always were. Your loyalty to mortals will be your undoing. And Cassian… he is a fool. He will fall as well. Tonight, the true power will be mine."

He intensified his mental assault on Lyra, the pull becoming agonizing. Lyra felt her consciousness wavering, her will threatening to snap. The images of her family, of her vengeance, of Cassian's bewildering tenderness, flashed through her mind, a maelstrom of conflicting emotions.

Just as Lyra felt herself beginning to yield, a thunderous roar echoed from the tunnel behind Arkyn. The ground trembled, and the air crackled with a sudden, overwhelming surge of raw power.

Cassian.

He burst into the cavern, his clothes torn, blood on his face, but his golden eyes blazing with an unholy fury. He was a whirlwind of dark vengeance, his powerful form radiating an aura of devastating strength. He had fought his way through the chaos, through the collapsing castle, to reach her.

"Arkyn!" Cassian roared, his voice thick with unbridled rage. "You will not touch her!"

Arkyn's composure finally broke. His eyes widened, a flicker of genuine shock in their depths. He hadn't anticipated Cassian's swift arrival, his overwhelming fury. The surprise was enough.

Cassian lunged, moving with a speed that defied the eye, a direct assault fueled by fury and a desperate need to protect Lyra. Arkyn, momentarily caught off guard, raised his hands, a shield of dark energy shimmering around him.

The clash was instantaneous, a blinding explosion of raw power that ripped through the cavern. The very stones screamed, and a wave of force slammed into Lyra, throwing her back against the tunnel wall. She hit it with a sickening thud, her vision blurring, darkness encroaching.

The last thing she saw before consciousness threatened to leave her was Cassian, locked in a brutal, desperate battle with Arkyn, a clash of ancient titans, fighting for her, for control, for the very soul of Sinful Castle. The undoing had truly begun. And Lyra, unconscious, but still defiant, was at its fiery heart.

Chapter 26: The Throne Isn't Empty

Lyra awoke to the searing pain of her body slamming against stone, and the distant, echoing roar of battle. Her head throbbed, and her vision was a dizzying kaleidoscope of black and red. She pushed herself up, every muscle screaming in protest, her hand instinctively going to her throbbing temple.

The cavern was a maelstrom of chaos. Cassian and Arkyn were locked in a brutal, incandescent struggle at the heart of the chamber, their forms blurring into streaks of dark energy and flashing gold. Ancient magic crackled around them, ripping through the very air, shaking the bedrock of the castle. The sounds of their clash – guttural snarls, the rending of ancient magic, the impact of blows that resonated through the earth – were deafening.

Lorcan was there too, defending the terrified offerings. He moved with a quiet, lethal grace, deflecting stray bursts of Arkyn's power, guiding the girls deeper into the less volatile tunnels. His twilight eyes, however, kept darting back to the titanic struggle between his brothers, a profound concern etched on his face.

Lyra forced herself to her feet, leaning heavily against the rough stone wall. The map, still tucked securely in her pocket, was a constant, burning reminder of her purpose. She scanned the cavern, her mind racing despite the pain. Cassian and Arkyn. Two forces, two ancient powers, pitted against each other.

Arkyn, cloaked in shadows that seemed to coil and writhe, attacked with cold, precise malice, aiming to disable and dominate. Cassian, however, fought with a raw, almost feral fury, a protective rage that seemed to amplify his already immense strength. He wasn't fighting for power, Lyra realized. He was fighting for her.

A blinding flash of energy erupted from the center of the cavern as Cassian unleashed a devastating surge of golden light, pushing Arkyn back. Arkyn roared, momentarily stunned, his shadowy form flickering. It was Lyra's chance.

"Lorcan!" Lyra yelled, her voice raw, but cutting through the din. "The ceremonial chamber! Arkyn's ultimate goal!"

Lorcan's head snapped towards her, his eyes widening in understanding. He knew the significance. He had provided the map. He pointed to a small, almost invisible crevice in the cavern wall, deep within the shadows. "That way, Lyra! It leads directly to the core ritual chamber! Cut off his power source!"

Lyra nodded, her gaze fixed on the crevice. This was the heart of Arkyn's ambition, the place where he intended to harness the "Blood of the Unbroken." If she could disrupt it, sever his connection, she might just give Cassian the edge he needed.

She started towards it, scrambling over rubble and dodging stray bursts of energy. Her body screamed with pain, but her resolve was iron. She heard Cassian roar her name, a desperate warning, as Arkyn, regaining his footing, unleashed a wave of dark magic aimed directly at her.

"No!" Cassian bellowed, diverting his attack, throwing himself between Lyra and Arkyn's assault. The force of the blow slammed into Cassian, sending him hurtling back against a jagged rock formation with a sickening crunch. He cried out, a raw, guttural sound of pain, his form momentarily flickering.

"Cassian!" Lyra screamed, her heart seizing in her chest. Arkyn had seized the opportunity, his eyes burning with renewed triumph. He began to draw a new surge of dark energy, clearly aiming to finish Cassian.

Lyra knew what she had to do. Cassian was fighting for her, protecting her. Now, she had to fight for him. And for them all.

She reached the crevice. It was narrow, just wide enough for her to squeeze through. She looked back at Cassian, struggling to rise, Arkyn's power already building towards him. Lyra knew he would sacrifice himself for her. But she wouldn't let him.

"You won't have him!" Lyra roared, her voice ringing with defiance. She squeezed through the crevice, plunging into the darkness beyond.

The tunnel was short, leading directly into a small, circular chamber, clearly the core ritual room. It was austere, with ancient symbols etched into the floor, radiating a cold, dark power. In the center, suspended in the air by invisible forces, was a shimmering, pulsating orb of black energy – Arkyn's power source, his connection to the ancient magic he was trying to corrupt.

Lyra didn't hesitate. She pulled the dagger from its concealed garter, the cool steel a familiar weight in her hand. This blade had been intended for Cassian, but now, it had a different purpose.

She lunged towards the orb, ignoring the wave of oppressive magic that tried to push her back. Her eyes fixed on the pulsating black heart of Arkyn's ambition. She wouldn't just disrupt it; she would shatter it.

Just as her hand reached the orb, a chilling voice echoed from behind her, filled with ancient triumph. "Too late, little mortal. The ritual is complete. The power is mine."

Arkyn stood in the doorway, his eyes blazing with cold victory, a malevolent smile twisting his ancient features. He had left Cassian to Lorcan and the others, knowing Lyra would come directly to this chamber. He had underestimated Cassian, but he had correctly anticipated Lyra's next move.

"The power of the Unbroken is now woven into my essence," Arkyn purred, his voice resonating with a terrifying strength. "You are merely the catalyst. The key. And now… you are mine. To command."

He extended his hand, not to attack, but to exert control. Lyra felt an invisible current, a horrifying invasion of her mind, her will. It was Arkyn's magic, attempting to bind her, to transform her, to possess her as his ultimate vessel. Her blood rebelled, the essence of the Unbroken fighting back, but it was a desperate, losing battle against his ancient power.

Just as Lyra felt her consciousness begin to slip, a familiar voice, raw with desperation and power, ripped through the chamber. "She is not yours, Arkyn!"

Cassian. He burst into the chamber, wounded but furious, his golden eyes blazing with an unholy light. He was battered, bleeding, but his power was immense, fueled by a rage Lyra had never witnessed.

Arkyn snarled, turning to face Cassian. "Fool! You cling to a mortal? A mere vessel?"

"She is more than a vessel!" Cassian roared, his voice thick with protective fury. He launched himself at Arkyn, not with a calculated attack, but with a raw, desperate surge of power. He knew he couldn't beat Arkyn at his own game, not while he was linked to the ritual orb. But he could break the link.

Cassian didn't aim for Arkyn. He aimed for the pulsating orb. With a desperate, powerful blow, he slammed his fist into the shimmering black energy.

A blinding explosion ripped through the chamber. The orb shattered, sending fragments of dark magic screaming into the air. The ancient symbols on the floor erupted in crackling, malevolent light, then faded into dust. Arkyn roared in pain and fury, his connection severed, his power abruptly draining.

The surge of magic hit Lyra with a violent force, throwing her against the wall once more. She felt a searing pain, then a dizzying blackness. Her last conscious thought was of Cassian, a desperate, defiant shield against the darkness. He had chosen her over the very power Arkyn sought. He had chosen to destroy the source of his potential dominion to save her.

He had refused the throne, the ultimate power, to save Lyra. The chamber, once pulsing with Arkyn's ancient ambition, was now silent, the echoes of battle fading. The throne, Lyra realized, wasn't empty. It was broken. And Cassian had broken it for her.

Chapter 27: His Bite, My Undoing

Lyra awoke to silence. Not the oppressive, heavy silence of the castle, but a quiet, almost peaceful stillness. Her head still throbbed, a dull ache reverberating behind her eyes, but the dizziness had subsided. She opened her eyes slowly, the ancient stone ceiling of the cavern swimming into view.

She was no longer lying on the rough floor. She was cradled against something warm, solid, and undeniably powerful. Cassian.

He was sitting with his back against the cavern wall, holding her gently in his arms. His face was etched with exhaustion, dried blood smeared across his cheek, but his golden eyes, though weary, were clear and fiercely protective. He looked down at her, a profound relief washing over his features.

"Lyra," he murmured, his voice hoarse, thick with emotion. He reached up, his thumb gently brushing a strand of hair from her face. "You're awake."

Lyra's gaze swept over the chamber. The pulsating orb of dark energy was gone, shattered. The ancient symbols on the floor were faded, inert. Arkyn was nowhere to be seen. The oppressive magic, the chilling sense of manipulation, had vanished, replaced by a lingering coolness in the air.

"Arkyn?" Lyra whispered, her voice weak.

Cassian's jaw tightened. "He fled. Wounded. His power severely diminished. He will not trouble us again for a long time. Perhaps never." His eyes held a grim satisfaction. "You saved us, Lyra. You gave me the opening. You cut off his source."

Lyra looked at him, then at her own hand, which still clutched the hilt of the dagger, her knuckles white. The blade that had nearly taken his life had ultimately saved them both. The irony was profound.

"And you," Lyra said, her voice catching slightly. "You chose to destroy it. The source of his power. Of… a throne." She remembered his desperate, powerful blow, his choice to shatter the orb to protect her. "You refused the throne. For me."

A faint, almost tender smile touched Cassian's lips. "Some thrones are not worth the price. And some bonds are more powerful than any dominion." He looked at her, his golden eyes filled with an intensity that took her breath away. "My undoing, Lyra Virellan. You called it. You are it."

Lyra felt a strange mix of emotions churn within her. Relief that Arkyn was gone. Exhaustion from the battle. And a bewildering, undeniable tenderness for the powerful vampire who held her so carefully. The hatred that had once defined her was utterly gone, replaced by a complex tapestry of gratitude, respect, and a profound, aching desire.

She looked at him, truly looked at him, beyond the monster, beyond the captor, beyond the savior. She saw Cassian. Wounded, exhausted, but fiercely devoted. He had battled his own brother, risked everything, for her. The lines between their worlds, between their species, had blurred into nothingness.

Lyra reached up, her fingers tracing the dried blood on his cheek, then the faint scar beneath his jaw. The wound he carried, the story he hadn't fully told. He had sacrificed for her, protected her, believed in her. He had shown her a side of himself that no one else had seen.

"Cassian," Lyra whispered, her voice raw with a newfound understanding. "The hatred… it's gone. Arkyn… he tried to make me hate you. To make me a weapon against you. But it's gone. Replaced by… something else." Her gaze dropped to his lips, stained faintly with her blood from the final kiss before the battle. The taste of him, of their shared power, lingered.

His golden eyes darkened, reading the unspoken words in hers. He knew what she was admitting. The profound shift. The terrifying, bewildering surrender of her heart.

He leaned in, his breath warm against her face. "What is it, Lyra?" he murmured, his voice husky with anticipation. "Tell me."

Lyra lifted her head, meeting his gaze fully. The last vestiges of her resistance, of her carefully constructed walls, crumbled. She had fought against it, struggled against it, but it was undeniable. The thirst she felt now was not for vengeance, but for him.

"It's... you," Lyra confessed, her voice barely audible. "Only you."

A profound, almost overwhelming wave of emotion washed over Cassian's face – relief, triumph, and an ancient, aching devotion. His hand came to cup her jaw, his thumb gently stroking her skin.

"Then let it be so," he whispered, his golden eyes blazing with a fierce, possessive tenderness. "Let your undoing be mine."

He lowered his head, not to her lips, but to her neck. Lyra felt her heart quicken, a thrilling anticipation coursing through her veins. This wasn't a bite of a test, or a punishment, or even a desperate feeding. This was different. This was a choice. Her choice.

She tilted her head, exposing the sensitive skin of her throat, offering herself freely. Her fingers reached up, tangling in his dark hair, pulling him closer. There was no fear now, only an exhilarating, profound willingness.

His fangs pierced her skin, a sharp, exquisite pressure that sent a jolt through her, followed instantly by the familiar, yet utterly unique, wave of euphoric bliss. This time, there was no pain, only the dizzying, intoxicating pleasure that flooded her senses, dissolving all thought, all memory, until only Cassian remained. She felt herself drawn into him, her essence mingling with his, a powerful, unbreakable bond forming in the deepest parts of her being. It was a complete, willing surrender, a merging of souls, forged not in chains, but in undeniable desire.

She felt him draw deeply, rhythmically, pulling her closer, absorbing her, making her a part of him. And Lyra, lost in the overwhelming tide of sensation, pressed herself against him, craving more, giving everything. This was not being taken. This was giving. This was her choice.

He pulled back, slowly, reluctantly, his fangs disengaging with a soft, intimate sound. Lyra gasped, her eyes fluttering open, filled with the hazy afterglow of blissful saturation. She felt utterly depleted, yet profoundly complete, whole. The bite mark on her neck throbbed, a hot, aching pulse, but it was a mark of belonging, a brand of love, not ownership.

Cassian looked at her, his golden eyes dark with satiated hunger, but now brimming with an overwhelming tenderness. He lowered his head, pressing a soft, lingering kiss to the wound, then looked up at her, a profound declaration in his gaze.

"My Queen," he murmured, his voice husky, filled with a raw, ancient devotion.

Lyra, still breathless, gazed at him. His bite, once a symbol of her intended undoing, had become the very thing that liberated her, that brought her to this profound, terrifying, and utterly beautiful realization. **His bite, her undoing.** And in that undoing, she found a new, unexpected beginning. A path she had never foreseen, forged in blood, defiance, and a love that had blossomed from the ashes of hatred.

Chapter 28: The Girl Who Walked Into Hell

The world slowly sharpened into focus, the intoxicating haze of Cassian's bite receding to leave Lyra feeling paradoxically both utterly sated and fiercely alive. She lay nestled against him, the cavern silent save for their quiet breaths. The mark on her neck throbbed with a comfortable warmth, a silent testament to a bond forged not of force, but of choice.

He held her, his strong arms a secure cage around her, yet she felt unbound, truly free for the first time in her life. The vengeance that had fueled her, the hatred that had consumed her, had been replaced by a new, bewildering clarity. Cassian, the monster she'd come to destroy, was now her anchor, her unexpected solace.

"We need to find Lorcan," Lyra murmured, her voice still a little hoarse from the aftermath of the bite. She stirred, trying to sit up, but Cassian's grip tightened gently, keeping her close.

"He will find us," Cassian replied, his voice deep, his lips brushing against her hair. "He is resourceful. And he knows his way through the shadows better than any." He kissed her forehead, a soft, tender gesture that made her heart ache with a strange, beautiful emotion. "Rest, Lyra. The worst is over."

But Lyra knew the worst was far from over. Arkyn had fled, wounded, but a wounded predator was still dangerous. And the castle… the castle was still a labyrinth of power and fragile alliances.

As if on cue, a soft scuffling sound echoed from one of the side tunnels. Lyra tensed, but Cassian merely shifted, pulling her closer, his gaze fixed on the opening.

Lorcan emerged, his dark clothes dusty, but his posture as composed as ever. Behind him, huddled together, were the offerings, their faces still pale but now etched with a fragile hope. They looked disoriented, but alive. He had saved them.

Lorcan's twilight eyes scanned the cavern, settling first on Cassian, then on Lyra, still cradled in his arms. A flicker of relief, quickly masked, crossed his features. He saw the new depth in their connection, the intimate aftermath of the bite, and understood its profound significance.

"Brother," Lorcan said, his voice quiet. "The loyalists have secured the main hall. The fire is contained. Arkyn's forces are scattered. He is weakened, but he still poses a threat."

Cassian nodded, his jaw tight. "He will be hunted. He will answer for his treachery." He looked down at Lyra, a silent question in his golden eyes.

Lyra gently pushed herself up, breaking free from Cassian's embrace. She felt a strange surge of strength, a clarity of purpose that hadn't been there before. The bite, instead of weakening her, had awakened something new within.

She walked towards Lorcan and the offerings, her posture regal despite her exhaustion, the crimson dress a stark, defiant splash of color against the stone. The offerings, seeing her approach, parted instinctively, their gaze fixed on her with a mixture of fear and awe.

Lyra stopped before them, her eyes sweeping over each frightened face. She remembered their terror, their helplessness, the desperate hope in their eyes during the selection. She remembered Melina, broken by fear. She remembered her own journey, from a pawn of vengeance to a catalyst for change.

"You are safe," Lyra stated, her voice clear and strong, resonating through the cavern. "Arkyn's ritual is undone. His power is shattered. You are free."

A wave of bewildered relief washed over the offerings. Some wept silently, others simply stared, too stunned to react.

"But this is not merely freedom," Lyra continued, her gaze unwavering. She looked at Lorcan, then back at the offerings. "This castle… this world… it has been ruled by fear and manipulation for too long. Arkyn's thirst for power corrupted everything. It twisted our very existence."

She turned, her gaze sweeping over the silent, watchful figures of Cassian and Lorcan, then back to the offerings. "I walked into this hell with one purpose: vengeance. To destroy the monster who took my family. But the monster was not who I thought. The monster sought to control everything, to enslave even the will. And that monster is broken."

Her eyes blazed with a fierce conviction. "You were meant to be owned. To be consumed. To be molded into something you are not. But you are not. You are *unbroken*." She looked at each girl, her gaze holding a profound empathy. "You survived. You endured. You witnessed true power, and you refused to be extinguished."

Suddenly, one of the offerings, a shy girl with trembling hands, slowly, tentatively, sank to her knees. Then another. And another. Soon, all of the offerings, their faces streaked with tears and dirt, were kneeling before Lyra. Not in submission, but in a profound gesture of respect, of gratitude.

Lyra looked at them, a wave of emotion washing over her. She was not a queen. She was not a goddess. She was just a mortal girl who had walked into hell. But she had seen something in them, something unbroken, that they had not yet seen in themselves. And they, in turn, saw something in her.

Cassian, who had approached and now stood a few feet behind Lyra, watched the scene unfold, his golden eyes filled with a deep, silent pride. Lorcan, too, watched, a rare, soft smile gracing his lips.

Lyra bent down, gently helping the first girl to her feet. "Rise," she commanded, her voice soft but firm. "You kneel to no one. Not anymore." She helped another, and another, until all the offerings were standing, looking at her, their faces filled with a new, quiet strength.

"The rules of this castle are rewritten," Lyra declared, her voice resonating with a newfound authority that surprised even herself. "The age of absolute control is over. The age of choice begins."

She looked at Cassian, her eyes holding a silent promise. He had called her his undoing. But in her undoing, he had also found his own. And together, they would rebuild. Not a throne, but a future. The girl who walked into hell had not only survived, but had emerged, not as a victim, but as a beacon of resistance, the queen of the unbroken.

Chapter 29: Ashes of What I Was

The immediate aftermath of Arkyn's defeat and Lyra's defiant emergence was a whirlwind of activity. Cassian, battered but victorious, began the arduous task of securing the castle and solidifying his new, tenuous reign. Lorcan, ever the strategist, moved with quiet efficiency, organizing the loyalists and ensuring the safety of the freed offerings. The atmosphere in Sinful Castle, though still tense, was now charged with a nascent sense of possibility, a fragile hope for a future free from Arkyn's tyranny.

Lyra found herself moving through it all with a strange detachment. Her body was healing, the bite marks on her neck now faint, almost invisible, but humming with a deep, internal resonance that bound her irrevocably to Cassian. The emotional scars, however, were still raw. The years of hatred, the singular focus on vengeance, had defined her. Now, that purpose was gone, replaced by a bewildering array of new responsibilities, new alliances, and a love she never anticipated.

She spent the following days tending to the other offerings. Many were still traumatized, their spirits fragile. Lyra spoke to them, not as a leader, but as one who had shared their fear, their pain. She helped them navigate the castle's hidden passages, ensuring they could leave if they wished, or find safe havens if they chose to stay. She saw the relief, the burgeoning strength in their eyes, and a quiet satisfaction bloomed in her heart. This was her new purpose, a different kind of fight.

One evening, as the last vestiges of twilight faded from the sky, Lyra found herself alone in what used to be her and Cassian's shared chambers. He was occupied with the endless demands of reorganizing the vampire court. The room, once a gilded cage, now felt strangely empty, filled with the echoes of a past self she barely recognized.

She walked to the ornate fireplace, where a low fire crackled, casting dancing shadows on the walls. Her gaze fell on a small, exquisitely carved wooden box on a nearby table – the same box Lorcan had held, the one that had contained the dried flower and the map of hidden passages. The map was now safe, its purpose served. But the box…

Lyra picked it up. She remembered her first encounter with Lorcan, his cryptic warnings, his subtle guidance that had led her to the truth. She remembered finding her family's fate, the cruel manipulation of Arkyn, written in his ledgers. She remembered the fire, the chaos, and the choice she had made.

She opened the box. Inside, the dried flower still rested on its bed of faded velvet. It was a simple, delicate bloom, long since deprived of life, yet holding a poignant beauty. It symbolized everything she had been: the memories, the grief, the burning desire for vengeance, the rigid purpose that had defined her.

She closed her eyes, taking a deep breath. The scent of woodsmoke mingled with the faint, persistent scent of Cassian that clung to the room. The memories flooded her: her parents' faces, blurred by time, then sharpened by the raw, vivid pain of their loss. The cold resolve that had consumed her. The endless training, honing herself into a weapon. The moment she had walked into Sinful Castle, a lamb willingly entering the lion's den, blade hidden, heart filled with singular hatred.

That girl. The Lyra Virellan consumed by vengeance. She was gone. Shattered by truth, reshaped by an unexpected love, and now burdened by a new, vast responsibility.

She opened her eyes. With a slow, deliberate movement, Lyra took the dried flower from the box. She held it for a moment, letting the last echoes of her past self resonate within her. Then, with a profound sense of release, she walked to the roaring fireplace.

She didn't hesitate. With a whisper of farewell to the girl she once was, Lyra dropped the dried flower into the hungry flames.

The delicate petals curled, caught fire instantly, and dissolved into a shower of bright, ephemeral sparks, then vanished into fine gray ash. It was a swift, silent cremation, a symbolic letting go. The last physical vestige of her past purpose, her singular hatred, turned to nothingness.

Ashes of what I was, she thought, a profound sense of emptiness, yet also a burgeoning freedom, settling over her. The vengeance was gone. The hatred, burned away. And in its place, a space opened for something new to grow.

She walked back to the box, placing it empty on the table. It was a reminder now, not of what she had to do, but of what she had *overcome.*

Just then, Cassian entered. He stopped, his golden eyes sweeping over the room, then landing on Lyra, standing by the fireplace, her face illuminated by the flickering flames. He saw the quiet intensity in her eyes, the subtle shift in her aura. He sensed the profound change within her.

He walked to her, his movements silent, powerful. He didn't speak. He simply reached out, his hand gently cupping her face. His thumb brushed over her cheek, a soft, comforting touch.

"What troubles you, Lyra?" he murmured, his voice low, filled with a deep understanding. He looked into her eyes, truly seeing her, seeing the aftermath of her symbolic act.

Lyra met his gaze, her heart filled with an unexpected tenderness. "I... burned it," she confessed, her voice soft, a hint of emotion in her tone. "The last piece of who I was. The vengeance. The girl consumed by hatred." She gestured towards the fireplace, where only faint ash remained. "It's gone. All of it. And I don't know... what remains."

Cassian's lips curved into a soft, understanding smile. He pulled her gently into his arms, holding her close. His body was warm, solid, a steady anchor against her vulnerability.

"What remains, Lyra Virellan," he whispered, his voice deep and resonant, "is everything. Strength. Courage. A fire that can ignite hope, not just destruction. And a heart that has found its truth, even in the darkest of places." He pressed a kiss to her hair, then to the mark on her neck. "You are not empty, my Lyra. You are... reborn. Forged in fire, bound by choice."

Lyra leaned into him, feeling the truth of his words settle deep within her. The ashes of her past were scattered, yes. But from those ashes, something new was rising. A queen, perhaps. Not of a throne, but of a broken world, ready to be rebuilt. And with Cassian by her side, guiding her, protecting her, she knew she could face whatever came next. The undoing was complete. And the phoenix was ready to rise.

Chapter 30: The Queen of the Unbroken

Days bled into weeks, and weeks into a new, fragile era for Sinful Castle. The ashes of Lyra's past, scattered into the fireplace, felt like a powerful liberation. The castle, once a monument to tyranny and hidden rituals, was slowly, painstakingly being reshaped. Cassian, with Lorcan as his quiet, indispensable strategist, worked relentlessly to stabilize the court, to quell the last whispers of Arkyn's loyalists, and to begin the monumental task of rebuilding trust.

Lyra was no longer confined to Cassian's chambers, though she often chose to be there. She moved freely through the castle, a quiet force of change. She continued to work with the freed offerings, helping them find their footing in a world that had tried to break them. Some chose to return to the mortal world, scarred but free. Others, drawn by a strange sense of belonging, by the protection offered by Cassian and the hope Lyra embodied, chose to remain, cautiously hopeful for a new life within the vampire domain.

Her relationship with Cassian had deepened into something profound and undeniable. It was a bond forged in battle, in shared secrets, and in the bewildering, intoxicating acceptance of a love that defied all logic. He was still the powerful, possessive vampire, but his possessiveness now stemmed from a fierce devotion, not just a predatory instinct. His golden eyes, once filled with a dangerous amusement, now held a constant, tender watchfulness whenever she was near. He never spoke of "ownership" again. He spoke of partnership, of a shared future.

One evening, as the twin moons of the vampire world cast their silvery glow through the high windows of the grand hall, Cassian found Lyra standing in its very center. The hall, though still bearing the scorch marks of the fire and the lingering scent of battle, felt different. Cleaner. Lighter. The oppressive magic was gone, replaced by a sense of calm.

Cassian approached her, his footsteps silent on the polished marble. He was clad in simpler, yet still regal, dark attire, devoid of the heavy robes he once wore. He looked less like a lord of war and more like a king in quiet command.

"The last of Arkyn's remaining factions have been dealt with," Cassian announced, his voice low, his golden eyes filled with a weary satisfaction. "The castle is secure. The court… is beginning to find its new rhythm."

Lyra turned to him, a faint, soft smile touching her lips. "And the offerings?"

"Those who wished to leave have gone, escorted to safety," he replied. "Those who remain… are being cared for. Lorcan has established new protocols, ensuring no such ritual will ever be conceived again."

He walked towards her, stopping inches away, his presence warm and comforting. He reached out, his hand gently cupping her face, his thumb tracing the line of her jaw. His gaze was intense, filled with a raw, ancient tenderness.

"And you, Lyra Virellan," he murmured, his voice husky. "What of you? You walked into hell for vengeance. You burned it down for freedom. What remains for you now?"

Lyra met his gaze, her heart filled with a profound peace she hadn't known was possible. The past was truly ashes. The future, once a terrifying blank, now stretched before them, a canvas waiting to be painted.

"I am not a slave, Cassian," Lyra said, her voice clear and strong. "I am not a concubine. And I am not just a… companion." She paused, her eyes holding his, a quiet understanding passing between them. "I am Lyra Virellan. The girl who refused to break. The last of the Unbroken."

A slow, profound smile spread across Cassian's face, his golden eyes gleaming with pride and something akin to awe. He knew what she was saying. He knew what she was choosing.

"You are more," Cassian declared, his voice deep and resonant, a vow echoing in the quiet hall. "You are the embodiment of everything Arkyn sought to destroy, and everything he could never possess. You are the courage they will look to. The defiance they will remember. You are the light in our shadows."

He reached out, taking her hands in his, his gaze unwavering. "Be my queen, Lyra Virellan," he said, his voice a solemn promise, laced with a raw, undeniable devotion. "Not of a crumbling throne, but of a new era. A new kind of rule. With me. By my side. Not beneath me, but with me, equal. My partner. My... everything."

Lyra's breath hitched. Her heart swelled with an emotion so powerful it brought tears to her eyes. This was not the possessive claim of a monster, but the humble offering of a powerful being who had chosen her above all else. He was offering her not a crown, but a shared journey. Not dominion over others, but partnership in rebuilding. He had surrendered his own deep-seated need for control, for her.

"Yes, Cassian," Lyra whispered, her voice thick with emotion. "Yes."

He let out a low, triumphant sound, pulling her into a fierce, passionate kiss. His lips were warm, tasting of their shared history, of a future yet unwritten. It was a kiss of profound commitment, a merging of two worlds, two souls, bound by a love that had defied darkness, betrayal, and centuries of ancient power.

When he pulled back, Lyra was breathless, her eyes shining. She looked at him, truly seeing him now, not just as the powerful vampire, but as her king, her protector, her partner. And he, in turn, looked at her, his golden eyes alight with adoration, recognizing the fierce, unyielding spirit of the woman he loved.

Lyra Virellan, the girl who walked into hell seeking vengeance, had found her undoing in the heart of the monster. But in that undoing, she had found her true self. She had become the Queen of the Unbroken, not through conquest or fear, but through the power of choice, of compassion, and of a love that had defied all expectations. The throne wasn't empty. It was transformed. And Lyra, with Cassian by her side, was ready to rule.

Printed in Dunstable, United Kingdom